THE CASE OF THE SINISTER SPIRIT

JANE GALLOWS WITCH PRIVATE INVESTIGATOR BOOK 1

LEIGHANN DOBBS

LEIGHANN DOBBS PUBLISHING

SUMMARY

Jane Gallows isn't much of a witch. Her spells only work when she has a mouthful of chocolate, which can be downright awkward at times. That's why she makes her living as a private investigator.

Of course, being a P.I. has its difficulties too, not the least of which is her lazy, sarcastic cat, who insists he's the brains behind her sleuthing skills, and the ghost of a 1940s gumshoe that haunts her office and wants in on the case-solving action.

When old-timer Bud Saunders hires her to get rid of a ghost in his barn, she figures it will be a piece of cake. Not so much when he turns up dead that very day. Even worse, the sheriff wants to pin it on Jane.

Add in an unconventional family with a kooky cast of paranormal characters, a nosy neighbor who wants to turn them in for just about anything, and a witchy aunt who has suddenly gone rogue. Before Jane knows it, she's knee deep in a heap of trouble that even the most perfectly cast chocolate-laced spells can't solve.

CHAPTER ONE

The old man fidgeted in the chair across from my desk, twisting a dirty Red Sox baseball cap in his weathered hands. Sharp blue eyes assessed me from behind a leathery, wrinkled face. He leaned across the desk, his expression turning serious.

"I need your word that you'll keep my… err… problem… in the strictest of confidences."

"Of course, Mr. Saunders. I won't tell a soul."

"Call me Bud."

"Okay, Bud, what exactly is the problem?"

Bud held my gaze for a second then apparently decided I was trustworthy. "I think my barn is haunted, and I need you to get rid of the ghost."

That was the problem he needed kept in strict confidence? I had been expecting something juicier like an affair or embezzlement or maybe even a suspected murder, but haunted barns were par for the course in Hallows Crossing. Most people didn't even want to keep them secret.

In a town that boasted some of the bloodiest witch trials of the 1600s, most of the residents had figured out some kind of an angle to capitalize on the history. There were festivals and fairs and ghost walks, all designed to lure in tourists. And forget about Halloween. It was a madhouse around here.

"I don't want word to get out, though," Bud said. "Don't want no looky-loos and rubberneckers swarming my property."

"What do you think I can do to help?" I asked.

His eyes fell to the business card on the desk. Jane Gallows. Private Investigator. They flicked up to meet mine again.

"Well, don't you live in that big old house on the hill that looks like something from the set of *The Addams Family* and has all them kooks living in it?"

"Yep." It wasn't the first time I'd heard my relatives described as kooks. I didn't get offended because it was pretty much true. My family consisted of witches, ghouls and vampires, not to mention the odd assortment of pets they had around the house. They were a little bit eccentric but basically good people. Sure, my great-aunts liked to walk around wearing pointy witch hats sometimes, and my aunt and uncle slept in the family mausoleum, but in a town that attracted the eccentric, that didn't raise eyebrows among most people.

"Well then, you must be a witch, and witches can get rid of ghosts." Bud looked satisfied with his assessment of me.

I laughed. "I'm not a witch."

It was only sort of a lie. I really was a witch, just not a very good one. My limited witchy powers were somewhat hampered by the fact that my magic only worked if I was eating chocolate. Talk about inconvenient. And because of that, I'd flunked out of witch school and never fully developed my skills. I mean, one can only eat so much chocolate before one breaks out in zits and has to shop at the plus-size store.

His eyes narrowed. "Well, if you ain't up to the task, I suppose I could go to Mitch Pierce."

The mention of my ex's name was like an icy dagger to my heart. No way was I losing a client to him. I didn't care what I had to do. I wasn't sending any business over to my lying jerk of an ex. And besides, he wasn't a witch either, nor did he believe in ghosts.

"Oh no, I can help you." I'd successfully vanquished a few ghosts before, and I could always ask my cousins for pointers. "Why don't you tell me exactly what's going on."

Bud scowled. "It's enough to drive a man insane. Spooky lights in the night. Chains clanking. Moaning."

"And it's coming from your barn?"

"Yep, every single night. I haven't slept good in two weeks straight."

"I see."

"So you can do the job?"

"I believe so."

"Problem is I don't have very much money to pay you."

I sat back in my chair and let the silence hang between us. Why were all my clients broke? But if I didn't take the job, he'd go to Mitch, and I couldn't let that happen.

"We'll work something out."

A snore erupted from the sofa, and we both turned to see Jinx, my cat, lying on his back with all four legs splayed out, his large belly moving up and down as he snore-breathed.

"Did your cat just snore?"

"Yep."

"Weird."

That wasn't the only weird thing about the office,

but I wasn't going to tell Bud about the other thing.

Bud's eyes returned to mine. "So you gonna help me then?"

"Sure. I'll need to come by and check out the barn to see what's going on. What time is good?" Maybe the noise was just the barn settling. Or a light spirit that could be eradicated with some of my cousin's vanishing cream. If it was either of those, getting rid of it would be easy peasy.

Bud stood. "I live out on 242 Kenwick Road. I'll be home all day, but it'd be better if you waited until after dark. That's when the ghost comes out."

"It's not gonna be as easy as you think." The voice drifted out of the corner shortly before its owner appeared.

Did I forget to mention that my office had another occupant? Yeah, that was the *other* weird thing besides the snoring cat. My office had a ghost.

I should have known there was a reason the rent was so cheap. I'd figured it was because the place had been empty for seventy years and still had several old musty filing cabinets filled with yellowed case files shoved in the corner. Nope. Turns out the previous owner of those files also came with the space.

His name was Moe Sharpe. This had been his office back in 1948, before his private investigation career was cut short by a bullet from an angry husband right in this very office. Apparently Moe had liked the job so much his spirit had stayed in the office long after the body had been removed.

When I'd moved in, Moe had been practically giddy at the prospect of a new partner. Me, not so much. But no matter what I did—burning sage, chanting, even using my cousin's ghost vanishing cream—nothing got rid of him.

"Why is that?" I asked.

Jinx snorted and rolled over, his paws batting back and forth in some kind of a weird cat dream.

"That's the old Dunbuddy place up there on Kenwick Road," he said as if I should know what he was talking about. Moe actually could be helpful sometimes when it came to old town lore. He'd lived it. The problem was he often forgot that it was now almost a century later. I had no idea who the Dunbuddys were.

"So…"

Moe rolled his eyes, apparently exasperated with my lack of knowledge. "Well, see here, the problem is that you're not just dealing with a ghost. You're dealing with a ghost that buried a treasure."

Hmm… that could get dicey. "Treasure?"

"Yeah." He plopped into the chair and kicked his Florsheims up onto my desk. "You need to get all the facts before you accept a case. Every shamus knows that. Haven't I trained you properly?"

No. He hadn't trained me at all. I'd been a private investigator long before I had come to this office.

"You know how those treasure-hoarding ghosts are. They don't want anyone to dig up their cache," he continued.

He had a point. The treasure complicated things, but I was still pretty sure I could pull the job off. I wasn't going to renege no matter what. Bud would just go to Mitch, and I wasn't going to let that happen.

"I still think I can get rid of it." What I lacked in witch skills I made up for in P.I. skills. I was good at puzzling out the clues. I guess you could say that was my magic. And ghosts that lingered typically only did so because they had unresolved issues here on the physical plane. Once you resolved those issues, poof! They'd disappear.

Well, except for Moe, though maybe his unresolved issue was that he just didn't want to stop detecting. Anyway, I figured if I could puzzle out why the ghost was hanging around and solve the issue, he or she would disappear.

"Of course you can, Red."

I hated when he called me that. My hair was auburn, not red.

I grabbed my tote bag, disturbing Jinx, who rolled off the couch onto the floor. He leapt up, shook himself, and then looked around as if he totally intended to do that.

"What gives?" He scowled up at me, his face resembling that of an all-black Grumpy Cat with a white mustache.

"I'm going out. I got a job."

"For this you wake me up?" Jinx's expression turned sour, as if he'd eaten a day-old mouse.

"I thought you might want to come with me. I'm going to Tess's magic shop."

"Is that all?" He jumped back up onto the couch and curled into a tight ball. "You're on your own, kid. Call me when something interesting happens."

CHAPTER TWO

It was the kind of late-summer day on which the air was laden with warm sunshine and just a hint of fall. I decided to walk to Tess's a few streets over and enjoy the balmy weather. An added benefit was that the walk took me past Charming Chocolates. I needed to stop in and resupply.

I didn't have any magic without chocolates, so I always liked to keep them handy. Not to mention that I liked eating them. Either way, my frequent trips to Charming Chocolates had nothing to do with the fact that Joe Hayes, the chocolatier, was hotter than a bubbling witches' cauldron.

The doors chimed as I entered the shop and I was immediately immersed in the magical sensory experience of chocolate. The sweet, rich smell swirled around me as I looked into the cases filled with various assortments. Dark chocolate, light chocolate, white chocolate, marzipan, nonpareils. It was enough to make a girl swoon.

I stepped up to the counter, and Joe turned from where he was cutting penuche fudge. "Hey, Jane, what can I get you?"

Yes, we were on a first-name basis, but only because I came in here so often.

For a moment I was speechless as his gaze held mine. His eyes reminded me of the creamiest milk chocolate flecked with gold.

His brows rose slightly, and my cheeks heated as I realized he was waiting for me to give my order. "I'll have a bag of eyes. I mean maple creams."

"Good choice." Joe smiled and slid open the door of the display case, picking out the candies and popping them into a bag while I pulled out my wallet.

He came over to the register and handed me the bag. Our fingertips brushed against each other. I felt a little thrill of excitement. Was I imagining that he might have felt it too?

Probably, because the next thing he did was punch in the keys of the register, announce my total, and hold his hand out for the money. I guess it wasn't quite as thrilling for him.

I paid and turned to leave.

"I put something special in there for you, Jane. Sample of a new product."

I glanced down at the bag. "Thanks."

He smiled and then turned back to his task.

As I left the shop, I opened the bag. Inside, nestled among my maple creams, was a bigger piece of candy. Dark chocolate with white chocolate dots on the top. Was it a soft cream? What was inside? Coconut? Vanilla? I reached in to take it out—

"You better keep that Aunt Gladys of yours under control."

Vera Hightower, the head of the town council, blocked my way. I'd been so intent on looking inside the bag that I hadn't noticed her coming down the sidewalk. If I had, I would have dodged her by slipping into an alley or dashing to the other side of the street.

It was never pleasant running into Vera. She was always harping on my family. And while it was true that they did tend to get into some mischief, it was all very innocent. But Vera didn't see it that way. She saw everything that happened in town as something that could put a damper on tourism.

She scowled down at me with her perfectly coiffed blond hair and her pink Chanel suit.

"Did my aunt do something?"

"Yes, she did. She was over at Kellerman's Hardware buying up all the brooms. Why, there's hardly a broom left in the area. And you know the pre-Halloween festival is in two weeks, and how is that going to look when the tourists come and we don't have any brooms?"

"Umm…"

"I think she might have bats in her belfry."

Ha! The joke was on Vera. We actually did have bats in our belfry, but they were more like pets (yes, we actually had a belfry—no bell, however). I was a little worried about Aunt Glad though. Why would she be buying up all the brooms? That was odd behavior even for her. And though my aunts—actually my great-aunts—were getting up in age, they were still sharp as tacks. If Aunt Glad had been buying brooms, I was sure she had a good reason for it.

My grip tightened on the bag as Vera rambled on about how important it was for the town to bring in tourists. It was true the town lived and died by the tourism dollar, but I hardly thought having no brooms was going to scare them away.

Just one bite of chocolate and I could whammy her with a cat-got-your-tongue spell and shut her up. But I wouldn't do that. Magic wasn't to be used trivially. I waited for her to finish and then politely said, "I'll see what I can do about her."

I stepped to the side, hoping to brush her off and be on my way.

"You do that. But I'm going to be keeping a close eye on your family. Agnes Newman has reported some strange goings-on, and you don't want me to have to go to Sheriff O'Hara."

That was the last thing I wanted. Sheriff O'Hara and I didn't get along.

"No, ma'am," I said as I backed away from her. She gave me one last scowl and then turned to proceed on her way. I spun around and hurried down the street to Tess's magic shop.

Tess's magic shop, Divinations, was filled with the scent of incense and the twinkle of little white lights sprinkled amidst candelabras, spiderwebs, and pentagrams. Tess was in the back, dusting the crystal balls. Her corn-silk, waist-length blond hair swayed as she moved the pink feather duster back and forth.

She turned as she heard the door open, her smile fading when she saw my agitated state.

"Hey, Jane, what's wrong?"

"Ugh, I just had an altercation with Hightower."

She dropped the duster and came over to me. "Oh no. What did she want?"

"Apparently, Aunt Glad has been buying up all the brooms. Do you know anything about that?"

The door opened, and my other cousin, Liz, came in, her brown shoulder-length bob highlighting giant luminescent brown eyes. "I saw Hightower accost you down the street. I had to hide behind the Paul Revere statue in the park to avoid her myself. Did she want to vent about Aunt Glad?"

"Yeah. Do you know why?"

Liz nodded. "Seems she's having some problems with her flying skills."

Tess shrugged and waved her hand in the air. "Oh, I'm sure that'll all blow over. You know how she is."

The aunts were getting up there in years and had a few mixed-up spells, but broom flying was an essential skill that Aunt Glad had mastered ages ago. If she was having trouble with it, this could mean something more serious.

Tess's gaze dropped to the bag in my hand, and her face lit up. "Oh, did you visit that chocolatier hottie?" She waggled her eyebrows. "I'm surprised all the candy in that store doesn't melt when he's there."

"Yes, I bought some chocolates," I said, as if I had no interest in him other than buying chocolates. Because I didn't.

"Whatever. I think he likes you. You should totally go for it. It's been two years since you broke up with that viper Mitch, and you deserve a life."

"I'm not so sure about that." I really wasn't in the market to have my heart broken again, and besides, when it came to recommending potential dates, my cousins were not to be trusted. We'd spent a lifetime pulling pranks on each other in the love-interest department, like fixing each other up with duds or encouraging guys that one knew the other wanted to dump. Come to think of it, that was how I'd ended up with Mitch. He'd been a blind date they thought wouldn't take. Turned out they'd been right. Too bad it had taken me so long to realize it.

"She'll do it in her own time," Liz added. "Don't pressure her."

Tess made a face at Liz, and I smiled. My cousin's concern for me warmed my heart.

"I got a new client today," I said, changing the subject from my love life.

"Oh? Can we help?" Tess asked. I never used magic on any of my jobs unless it was to expedite the gathering of information. It was the witches' oath to not interfere with the outcome of the affairs of mortals, for one. And for another, I wanted to prove I could investigate better than anyone else. Especially Mitch. And besides, I didn't need magic. I was a pretty good investigator without it. I'd given Bud my word not to tell anyone about his problem, but my cousins didn't count.

"Don't tell anyone, but Bud Saunders says he has a ghost in his barn. Wants me to get rid of it." I pulled out the surprise chocolate and ate it. It was deliciously creamy, with a tinge of raspberry.

Liz's eyes narrowed. "Oh, the old Dunbuddy place."

"You know about it?"

"Yeah. Mary Dunbuddy was hanged as a witch in the 1600s. They say she bilked people out of their money and buried it on her property."

Liz would know. She ran the tours in Hallows Crossing, taking them through all the witch houses and the sites of the hangings and the stonings.

"But the Dunbuddy place isn't on my tour because there's never been any reporting of a ghost before."

"Huh, so a new apparition. Odd it would show up now."

Tess slipped behind the counter and perused the

shelves, pulling out a small white jar and handing it to me. "Take this. It's a new mixture I have for ghost vanishing cream. Put it on the doors and maybe that'll get rid of her. If she's not an old ghost, it should be easy to get rid of her."

I opened the jar and immediately gagged. It smelled like rotten eggs. "This would get rid of anyone."

Tess giggled. "I did use it on a guy I dated that wouldn't stop stalking me last week."

I put the cover back on quickly. "So the legend is true then? There is a treasure buried there?" I asked.

Liz shrugged. "That's just the legend. I doubt it. You know how things were back then. If someone did something someone else didn't like, people would just accuse them of witchcraft and let the mass hysteria get rid of them."

I nodded. Much like how Mrs. Newman was trying to accuse my family.

"But in reality, the person accused never usually did anything. That was probably the case with Mary Dunbuddy. Someone just wanted her out of the way. I doubt there's a treasure buried there." Liz pursed her lips. "Though there have been a couple of treasure hunters in town asking about the legend. But of course, I didn't tell them where the property was.

You'd have to go back pretty far in the town records to find it. It's changed hands a few times."

I looked down at the jar of cream in my hand. If Mary Dunbuddy had buried a treasure there, her ghost probably wasn't going to be scared off with a little vanishing cream. And if treasure hunters were seeking that treasure, that made the job more complicated.

"If you need any help, let us know," Tess offered. She must have also sensed that the job could get complicated and wanted to make sure I didn't get hurt. That was so like them. Ever since we were kids and I'd flunked out of witch school, they'd been protecting me. They had the best intentions, but I didn't need protecting.

I slipped the cream into my bag. "No, I think I'll be fine. I'll just pop over there tonight and check out the barn. If it gets sketchy, I'll let you guys know," I said.

I exited the shop and headed toward home. I had a few hours to kill before dark, and now was a perfect time to find out what was up with Aunt Glad and all those brooms.

CHAPTER THREE

"Alacazam… alacazooo!"

Clatter! Clang!

"Swishadoo!"

Clunk.

I cautiously made my way through the gothic furnishings in the family mansion toward the strange noises. Dark, deeply carved mahogany, red velvet, and chandeliers with cobwebs hanging from the prisms were everywhere. Some would have said the decor was outdated, but I was used to it. I'd lived here almost my whole life.

You might think it's a little odd that a grown woman of thirty-five still lives at home with her extended family, but technically I didn't live *with* my extended family. The mansion was where my aunts and uncles lived. I lived in the caretakers cottage. So in theory, I had my own place. It was much nicer, too, not stuffed with these clunky, overbearing antiques. I'd needed a place after the breakup, and since my parents were traveling around Europe, my great-aunts and -uncles needed looking after. It worked for us.

Clatter!

That had come from the patio. I veered in that direction.

The soft pitter-patter of feet beside me announced Jinx's arrival. How he'd gotten here from my office downtown I had no idea. Apparently he wasn't as lazy as he let on.

"What's up?" he asked.

"I'm checking out the strange noises on the patio."

"My food bowl's empty."

"Jinx, there could be an intruder. Is your food bowl all you can think about?"

"Pretty much." Jinx turned and headed toward the kitchen. "Can you fill it up when you're done?"

"Sure."

Out on the patio, Aunt Glad stood next to the pool, arms raised in front of her, brooms littering the cement at her feet. Her tight gray curls bounced like springs as she homed in on one of the brooms—a yellow plastic number—and wiggled her fingers at it.

"Ala-ka-zoo!"

The broom didn't budge.

"Aunt Glad, what are you doing?"

She turned to me, a sour expression on her face. "These brooms." She gestured wildly to the brooms scattered around. "They're lemons, all of them."

"But why do you have so many?"

"Old Bessie crapped out." She pointed to a battered wooden broom lying on one of the chaise lounges. "I'm trying out some newer models. But none of them seem to work." She turned and looked at me, a flicker of concern in her eye. "Least ways, I think it's the brooms."

"I'm sure it is." I looked doubtfully at the brooms. It wasn't the brooms so much that had the magic, it was the driver. But Aunt Glad knew that.

"Well, I hope so. You know how important it is to be able to fly the broom. And my brooming license is coming up for renewal. The notice with my test time should be coming any day now. What happens if I flunk the test? I won't be able to fly, and you know a witch is nothing without her broom..."

Her words trailed off, and she looked at me wide-eyed. "Oh dear, I'm so sorry. I mean, witches are fine without brooms. A broom isn't everything, you know."

My heart melted at her sympathetic concern. I'd never gotten as far as learning how to fly a broom in witch school. It didn't bother me though. Who wanted to fly around on a broom anyway? I had a car. It was faster, and it didn't mess up your hair as much.

I spotted movement over by the ten-foot-tall gothic fence that edged our property. "Why don't you go in the house, Auntie? I'll clean up out here."

Glad went toward the house, but instead of cleaning up, I headed toward the fence skirting the edge of the property. I had a suspicion as to what was going on out there.

I edged my way between some trees, taking a circuitous route toward where I'd seen the movement and coming in from behind. Just as I suspected, it was our next-door neighbor, Agnes Newman. She was crouched at the fence, binoculars in hand, a sprig of branches sticking out from the top of her beehive hairdo.

"What are you doing out here?"

She jumped and whirled around to look at me. "I know there's some shenanigans going on in there. Your family is unnatural. There is something odd going on here."

"That's not true. My family is just a normal, red-blooded American family."

"Really? Then what was your aunt doing with those brooms?"

"She's testing them out for the manufacturers to see which ones work best on concrete pool patios." Sometimes I surprised myself with how fast I could come up with these lies.

Mrs. Newman looked skeptical. "It didn't look like that to me."

I folded my arms over my chest, wishing I had some chocolates so I could cast a forget-about-it spell or maybe even a don't-come-around-here-no-more spell. But I didn't have any.

"You know you're trespassing. Your property line is over there." I pointed toward the woods. You could barely see the Newmans' house from where I was standing. It was another large estate that was set off in the distance. Even though we were standing at our fence, our property went well into the woods.

"You don't want me to call Sheriff O'Hara, do you?" I said. I avoided the sheriff as much as I could, but Mrs. Newman didn't know that.

"Well I never!" She jumped up and waddled off toward her house, clutching the binoculars to her chest. I noticed the well-worn trail that she took through the woods. This wasn't the first time Mrs. Newman had been spying through the fence. Maybe we should get dogs and let them patrol the perimeter.

I turned and went back into the house. In the kitchen, Aunt Wanda was at the sink, washing vegetables. Her long silvery hair gleamed in the fading sunlight.

"I don't know why you don't just use witchcraft on those vegetables," Glad said from her seat at the kitchen table.

"I like cooking." Wanda smiled at me. "Hey, Jane, are you coming for dinner?"

"I have to go meet with a client, but I can come back."

I joined her at the sink and helped her wash some carrots. The window above the sink looked out over the garden, where I could see Aunt Wanda's jack-o-lantern patch was in full bloom. As I watched, one of the jack-o-lanterns turned around and winked its lighted eye at me. It was midsummer, too early for normal pumpkins, but Aunt Wanda had special fertilizer. She even sold it at the farmer's market sometimes. And the jack-o-lanterns that grew in her garden all year long came in handy for all the town festivals.

"Was that Mrs. Newman I saw you talking to?" Wanda asked.

"Yep. She was spying."

"You want me to turn her into a toad?" Glad asked.

Wanda shook her head. "No. That would bring too many questions. We have enough of those already."

We were usually able to explain away all the odd behavior, clothing, and accessories by saying it was for my Uncle Cosmo's Halloween supply business. Skeletons, caskets, witches' hats, cauldrons, and even the bats were all part of the inventory. It worked out pretty well to satisfy people's curiosity. Well, other than Mrs. Newman's.

Aunt Wanda finished with the vegetables and went over to the cutting board. "We're having roast beef tonight. Henry and Lucretia are bringing a salad. Of course, we won't be eating till after the sun sets."

Henry and Lucretia, my aunt and uncle, lived in the mausoleum near the old family cemetery up on the hill. Yep, they were vampires and thus didn't come out during the daylight hours. Now you might think living in a mausoleum would be dirty, dusty, and uncomfortable with those cement crypts, but they had it fixed up pretty nice. Big-screen TV, comfortable chairs, and the caskets were lined with the softest down comforters. It almost looked like a little apartment—well, except for the ornate metal candelabras they used for lighting and the stone crypts in the middle of the room.

"Did you people forget about me?" Jinx cast angry glances at his food bowl.

I went to the cupboard and pulled out a bag of dry cat food.

"Not that crap. I want the canned stuff with the gravy."

"You only get that for treats," I said. "This stuff is healthier for you. You're getting a little fat."

"Look who's talking."

I glanced down at myself. I wasn't getting fat, was I? While I wasn't stick thin like my cousins, my stomach was still flat, and my hips still fit into my size tens.

I poured the kibble into the bowl. "Take it or leave it."

Schreeech!

We whipped around to see our housekeeper, Zelda, out in the hallway kicking the vacuum and unleashing a string of curse words in some foreign language.

The vacuum cleaner popped open, and dust and animal hair spilled out all over the floor.

"What's wrong with it?" Aunt Wanda asked.

"Ugh, this damn thing eez on the fritz. Squeals like a greased pig at the county fair then stops working."

Uncle Cosmo peered over the banister at the vacuum. His salt-and-pepper hair made him look distinguished, but the large screwdriver he held and the dirty T-shirt he wore ruined the effect. "Let me take a look. I heard that squeal upstairs."

He unscrewed the back of the vacuum cleaner. "Yep, here's the problem. This belt—it's wearing on one side and rubbing against the side of the vacuum. I'll just order a belt, and we'll be good to go."

Zelda put her hands on her hips and looked at the mess. "Well, how long eez that going to take?"

"I'll order it on Wal-azon. It'll be here in two days. I have primo shipping."

"Fine. What am I going to do about this mess in the meantime?"

"We have twenty brooms out on the patio. Maybe you could use one of those," Aunt Wanda said.

I heard a hissing noise and turned to see Jinx jerking his head toward the front door. "Come on, let's blow this popsicle stand. I want to check out that barn with you."

"You're coming with me?"

"Yeah, you might need some help, right?"

I didn't need any help, but I had to admit, even though Jinx was snarky and sarcastic, I enjoyed his company. I grabbed my bag and headed toward the front door.

"Don't be late for dinner. We're having it at eight sharp!" Aunt Wanda's voice drifted out the door after me.

CHAPTER FOUR

"You think there's any mice in this barn?" Jinx licked his lips as he eyed the large structure at the edge of Bud's property.

"Is that the only reason you came? For mice?" I'd wondered why he wanted to accompany me on the job. He wasn't usually this helpful.

Jinx managed to look offended. "Of course not. I want to help you. Really." He glanced back at the house, where we'd just been knocking on the door for a good ten minutes. "So where do you think the old guy is?"

Good question. He hadn't answered the door even though his truck was in the driveway. He'd said he'd be home all afternoon, but maybe he'd had to go out for something. I hoped it wasn't some sort of an emergency. Maybe he'd forgotten I was coming. But I was here now, and I could at least check out the barn and see if I could feel a ghostly presence.

I turned my attention to the barn, all dark and looming in the distance. "Maybe he's in the barn."

"Yeah, let's check that out." Jinx didn't wait for me. He trotted over then turned when he got to the door. "You coming or what?"

His face wasn't nearly as grumpy looking as usual. His sleek black fur gleamed in the moonlight, and the white markings on his upper lips that resembled a mustache twitched with the anticipation of fresh mice.

The barn door was edged about six inches open, revealing a black interior. Could ghosts open doors? I doubted that Bud kept the barn open. Maybe he was inside, though why would he be inside with the lights off?

I hesitated at the doorway.

"What are you, afraid?" Jinx taunted.

It wasn't so much that I was afraid, it was just that it was dark. I couldn't see and didn't want to trip over anything. Jinx, on the other hand, had excellent night vision and proceeded to run ahead inside. So much for wanting to help me out.

I stepped in. It was quiet other than the sound of Jinx's footsteps scurrying around in the corner. A mousey squeal of surprise was cut off abruptly with the sound of chomping and then a loud belch. Gross.

"Bud, you in here?"

Crickets answered. I stood still, inhaling the smell of dry hay and old wood and something else. I wasn't sure what the something else was. Maybe the ghost. If Bud wasn't here, I could at least try to conjure it and find out what I could do to get rid of it. Maybe I could even use the vanishing cream. If this ghost was newly manifesting, his or her skills would be minimal, and the cream would probably do the trick.

I closed my eyes and took a deep breath, waiting for the familiar tingle signifying an otherworldly presence to come, but nothing did. Liz had said there hadn't been any ghost sightings up here, but if the ghost was new to manifesting, the signal could be very weak. But if it was Mary, what had taken her so long? She'd been dead for centuries. What had she been doing all this time?

"Mary, are you in here? I can help you."

"I don't think she's here." Jinx's voice boomed from my left, scaring the crap out of me.

I stepped farther inside and pulled the ghost vanishing cream out of my purse. It would be pretty sweet to vanquish the ghost tonight and collect a modest fee from Bud. Heck, I wouldn't even charge much, and I'd let Bud work out an easy payment plan. It was only one night's work. The best part was that it was one night's work that Mitch wouldn't get. That was better than money.

I didn't know if the barn was wired with electricity, but I felt along the wall for some sort of switch anyway. "I need a light on in here." Not being able to see in the dark was going to be detrimental to smearing cream all over the place.

"No you don't," Jinx said. Easy for him to say; he had perfect night vision.

"Of course I do."

"Nope. Trust me."

"What are you talking about?"

"You don't see it?"

My eyes were getting more used to the darkness. I could see the individual stalls for the horses and bales of hay piled up here and there. But there was one lumpy thing in the corner that wasn't a bale of hay, and that was exactly where Jinx was looking. Was it the ghost? But I didn't sense a ghostly presence, and usually they were all misty and swirly, not dark and unmoving.

My private investigator skills kicked in. Something wasn't right about that lump. I inched my way over, reaching into my purse for my cell phone.

I pressed the flashlight app and aimed the beam at the lump. My heart jerked in my chest when I saw what the lump was. Bud Saunders wasn't going to be working out a payment plan. He was crumpled in the corner, pitchfork tines sticking through his chest.

Jinx looked up at me, his expression ominous. "I told you you didn't want to have a light on in here."

As much as I hated to do it, I had to call Sheriff O'Hara. Roberta O'Hara and I had had a venomous relationship since high school, when she'd accused me of stealing Mitch from her. I hadn't actually stolen him, as there had been nothing going on between the two of them, at least not on Mitch's side. But Bobby was fixated on him. You'd think that now, more than fifteen years later, she would have gotten over it, especially considering the louse he turned out to be, but nope. She still hated my guts.

Never mind that Mitch and I were no longer together. She was welcome to him, but it didn't seem to matter, so it was no surprise when she got out of her official car and eyed me suspiciously.

"You found a body?" she asked. The way she said

it made me think she wanted to replace the word "found" with "murdered."

I pointed to the barn and followed her in, careful not to look at Bud. It was disturbing.

"What were you doing out here?" Bobby asked as she slowly walked around the body.

"I had an appointment."

"For what?"

"He hired me."

Bobby glanced up from where she'd been crouched next to Bud's head and eyed me skeptically. "Really? You expect me to believe that."

"Yes."

"To do what?"

I suppose I could have told her. Having a ghost in your barn was really no big deal in Hallows Crossing. But legally, I didn't *have* to tell her. And I wanted to mess with her a little. "Sorry. Client–investigator privilege. Can't tell you."

She scowled at me, her face growing red. "Really? Then what's to make me think you didn't come here and have an argument with him and kill him?"

"Well, if I did that, do you think I would have called it in?"

She glanced from me to the body. "Maybe.

Maybe you called it in so as to divert suspicion from yourself."

"That seems stupid. No one's here. I could have just snuck off."

"We'll see about that. First, I'm going to have the medical examiner determine the time of death. Then you better hope you had an alibi." She was downright gleeful for a chance to pin a murder on me, no matter how slim that chance was.

The whole time we were talking, I tried to avoid looking at Jinx, who was perched on a bale of hay behind her, making faces at her. I couldn't really blame him. I wanted to make faces too.

"Looks like something scared the bejeezus out of him." Bobby aimed her flashlight at Bud's face, and I peeked out between the hands that were over my eyes. She had a point. His face was frozen in a grimace, his eyes wide open as if he'd seen something horrible. Like a ghost. But the pitchfork tines were coming through his chest from the back. If someone had stabbed him in the back, what had he seen in front of him that was so scary?

As I assessed the scene (it's scary how quickly one can get used to looking at a gruesome dead body), the puzzle pieces started to click into place. It was possible that no one had been behind Bud. If he'd been backing up, he could have tripped and fallen over one of the warped floorboards and impaled himself on the pitchfork.

"You think he was backing up and tripped?" I asked.

"I don't think so. Look at his face."

I tilted my head to get a better look at his expression. That grimace on his face might have just been surprise. "Maybe he was just surprised he tripped."

"Uh huh."

"You think someone stabbed him from behind?" Last I knew, ghosts couldn't wield pitchforks.

She started taking pictures, crouching again and tilting her head to the side to look at the wounds from all angles. Then she stood, stepped a few paces away from the body, turned, and studied it from afar.

"It's possible he did back up and fall on the pitchfork. This is all just preliminary. The medical examiner will know more, but looking at the angle of entry, it seems like someone would have had to be mighty tall to stab him with enough force to go through his chest. But if he fell, the weight of his body would have been enough to push the tines through."

"So it could have been an accident?" I asked, hopefully.

"Nope. Just falling wouldn't have been enough force. He was pushed. This was definitely murder."

"Murder!"

We wheeled around to see Vera Hightower standing in the doorway, her mouth agape. Her eyes, which flicked from the body to my face, darkened with suspicion. "I always knew you were no good, Jane Gallows. You and that weird family of yours. Now here's the proof." She gestured toward Bud's body.

"I didn't murder him. I just found him."

Vera glanced at Bobby for confirmation.

"That's what she says. She did call it in. At least that part is true," Bobby said.

It figured that Vera would show up. She was even nosier than Mrs. Newman. She considered it her duty to know everything that was going on in Hallows Crossing and monitored the police channel frequently, showing up at various crime scenes. Crimes could affect tourism.

"Darn it all! This murder could be bad for the festival!" Hightower wailed.

"Not to mention for Bud Saunders," I said.

Judging by the look on Bud's face, he'd been scared or surprised by something. My eyes darted around the barn. Had the ghost spooked him and caused him to trip? If so, it must be a very belligerent ghost.

This put me in a sticky situation. Should I still try to vanquish the ghost? Technically, I didn't have a client anymore, but I felt a little loyal to Bud now. I had given him my word. There was no chance of getting paid now, but I still felt I should follow through with the job.

"My squad will be here any minute. Vera, you don't need to be here. Jane, I want to get your statement, but not now. You'll have to come by the station later." Bobby said all this without looking up at us. "I don't want you people in here messing with the crime scene."

Jinx, still on the bale of hay, moved and distracted Bobby. She looked up at him. "Isn't that your cat, Gallows?"

"Nope. My cat has different markings."

"Traitor," Jinx said. Naturally, I was the only one that could hear him. I wasn't being a traitor though. I just didn't want anyone asking questions as to how my cat had gotten into the barn.

Bobby waved her hands at him. "Shoo, get out of

here. Go eat a mouse or something. I don't need you contaminating my crime scene."

Jinx presented her with his backside and then jumped down from the bale of hay and trotted off toward the door.

"Well, I guess I'll be going, too." I edged toward the door.

Bobby whipped around to scowl at me. "Yes, you can go. I'd say don't leave town, but I'd actually prefer it if you did. Wish that had happened decades ago."

I headed toward my car with Hightower on my heels.

"This stinks to high heaven, and I know your family has something to do with it. What were you doing in that barn, anyway?"

"What, are you on the police force now? I don't need to tell you what I was doing in there, but if you really need to know, I had an appointment with Mr. Saunders."

"Aha! You do have something to do with this. Does this have anything to do with your aunt and her brooms?"

"No. Leave my aunt out of this."

"Oh no, you're not going to weasel out of this one like you always do. I have Mrs. Newman on the case.

She's seen what goes on in that haunted house of a mansion you call home, and I promise you, if this death turns out to be something wonky that makes tourists cross our town off their vacation list, then I'm holding you accountable."

CHAPTER FIVE

"And you say he was deader than a headless zombie?" Uncle Cosmo looked up at me over the roast he was carving, his eyes brimming with equal measures of interest and concern.

"Undoubtedly." I took a roll and passed the basket to Liz.

"Who? Who? Who?" Hooter, the great horned owl that was a family pet, sat on his perch near the mahogany buffet table, his enormous round gold eyes demanding to know who we were talking about.

Aunt Wanda looked over at him. "Bud Saunders, if you must know."

Hooter blinked and executed a three-hundred-sixty-degree spin of his head. It always made my neck hurt when he did that.

"He's so nosy." Aunt Lucretia sopped up blood

from the meat tray with her roll, her white fangs slightly noticeable behind the slash of bloodred lips that made her pale face appear even more pasty.

"What did the pitchfork look like coming out of his chest? Was it bloody?" Aunt Glad sat at the end of the table, a pointy black-and-purple-striped witch hat sticking up on top of her head.

Wanda frowned at her. "Gladys, that's not a very nice question for dinner talk. And by the way, it's impolite to wear hats at the table."

Gladys's eyes turned upward. "Yeah, sorry about that. I was trying on these hats. It's new stock that Cosmo got in, and now if I take it off, I'll have hat hair." She lifted the hat a fraction of an inch to show us the flattened curls mashed into a triangle on the top of her head.

"Yeah, keep the hat on," Tess said.

"So what about the ghost? Did you get rid of it?" Liz asked.

"That's the funny thing. I didn't even sense a ghost there, but it sure looked like Bud had either been surprised or scared to death." I'd already told everyone that Bud had hired me to get rid of a spirit in his barn. Now that he was dead, I supposed I didn't have to keep it a secret. There would be plenty of looky-loos and rubberneckers swarming his property now with the rumors that were going to fly around. But Bud was beyond caring about that.

"Do you really think he was killed by a ghost?" Liz asked. "I'm just surprised there would be one at the barn. Because we haven't heard about that place being haunted, and most of the ghosts around here have been here since the 1600s."

Aunt Gladys made a face. "Did anyone in that area or anyone close to Bud die recently? Could be a new ghost."

I made a mental note to check on that. I'd been assuming the ghost was Mary Dunbuddy, but maybe it was someone else.

"Maybe it wasn't a ghost. Maybe it was that Charlie Henderson," Uncle Cosmo said.

"Who? Who? Who?" Hooter piped in.

"Charlie Henderson," Uncle Cosmo repeated more loudly. "Bud's next-door neighbor."

"Why would he kill Bud?" I was intrigued. I'd been working on the ghost theory, but maybe it hadn't been a ghost at all.

"They had a feud going," Uncle Cosmo said matter-of-factly. "Can someone pass the garlic green beans?"

Tess passed the plate in front of Uncle Henry, who jumped back in his seat and hissed.

"Sorry, Uncle Henry." Tess looked sheepish. "I always forget about your aversion to garlic."

"Smells like crap," Henry said, not surprisingly, considering he was a vampire.

"A feud?" I made another mental note.

"Oh yes, dear," Gladys said. "They were always messing with each other, trying to get each other's goat, you know." She pressed her lips together. "I thought it was mostly just in fun though."

My eyes drifted over to the window, looking in the direction of Agnes Newman's house. I guess one could say we had a feud with her too. She was always messing with *us*. In fact, she would have liked to see us gone for good. I didn't think she'd resort to murder, but maybe Charlie was more violent than Agnes.

"I guess we'll just have to let Sheriff O'Hara figure that out. Jane's not going to be looking into it. Her client is dead. Right, dear?" Aunt Wanda said.

It was true. Bud had hired me to find the ghost, and now that he was dead, I didn't have a client.

"Far be it from me to tell Jane what to do, but Sheriff O'Hara is only going to be looking at human suspects. If it really is a ghost that killed Bud, it's not a very nice ghost. It could be a deadly sinister spirit." Aunt Glad gave us all an ominous look.

Liz sighed. "And if it thinks killing someone by causing them to impale themselves on a pitchfork is fun, there's no telling what it will do next."

Vera Hightower's threat echoed in the back of my mind. If it was a spirit and it continued to act nasty, she was going to be all over me—and my family, especially Aunt Glad. Aunt Glad was keeping up a chipper conversation, but I could tell underneath she was truly worried about her problem with the broom. I didn't want to add to her worries.

But maybe I didn't have to get involved in a big investigation. If I could just smear some of the vanishing cream on the barn, the ghost might go away, and all our problems would be solved.

"I see those wheels turning, Jane," Uncle Cosmo said. "I admire your loyalty to your deceased client. Your parents always taught you to finish what you started. But if you're going to look into this, make sure you have plenty of chocolate. Whether the killer is otherworldly or not, you are dealing with someone dangerous who has already killed one person."

"Who? Who? Who?" Hooter flapped his great wings, and the twin tufts of fur on his head that resembled horns bristled like raised eyebrows as he craned his neck forward in my direction. His luminescent eyes stared at me, full of questions.

I stared back at him. "That, my friend, is a good question."

I helped my aunts clean up after dinner then headed to the stone cottage at the edge of the estate that I called home. I parted ways with Tess and Liz in the driveway. Tess headed toward the carriage house where she lived. Liz was the smart one; she had an apartment in town.

Jinx fell into step with me along the way.

"Where have you been?" I asked. Jinx hardly ever missed a family dinner, as Aunt Gladys was prone to feeding him scraps of meat from the table.

"If you must know, I was leaving Vera Hightower a present."

"A present? Thought you didn't like her."

"Can't stand her. This present wasn't the kind you're happy to get. Three little mouse heads lying right in a row on her stoop."

I probably should have admonished him. I couldn't get on board with killing innocent mice. Freaking out Vera Hightower, on the other hand, I approved of wholeheartedly.

"So, are you going to continue with the case?"

Jinx asked.

"Technically I don't have a case. No client."

Jinx scowled up at me. "What are you, some kind of quitter?"

We arrived at the stone cottage, and I stood on the steps in front of the large, round-topped oak door. Its giant iron hinges gleamed in the moonlight as I slid my oversized brass skeleton key into the lock. "I'm not a quitter."

"Then you have to keep working on the case. I heard Hightower's threat. Besides, you're not going to let O'Hara run amok with the suspects, are you? We probably left clues all over the barn that she'll try to use to frame us."

Jinx had a point. O'Hara was incompetent. Who knew what she would use in there to try to tie us to the murder?

I opened the door, and Jinx scooted through it in front of me. "Well, I suppose I could look into it a little."

Jinx trotted to the kitchen while I tossed my keys onto the side table. My place wasn't big, but it was comfortable. It had been built three hundred years ago as a caretaker cottage for the estate. The walls were all exposed stone, and an enormous stone fire-place with a hearth big enough to step inside dominated one wall. The windows were small with crosshatched panes, newly updated and energy efficient but still maintaining the old-world charm. I'd decorated in earthy tones of moss, amber, and red.

"Hey, what are you doing out there? I'm starving," Jinx yelled from the kitchen. "I've been running around all night finding mice to leave for Hightower. I think I deserve a treat."

I got the Fancy Feast out and slopped it into a bowl, and he immediately started gobbling it down.

While Jinx gorged himself, I plopped down on the overstuffed couch to think things over.

On the one hand, I wouldn't get paid for any investigation now that Bud was dead. But since I didn't have any other cases, I had nothing to do anyway.

Who knew what kinds of things we'd left in the barn? When I had been in there, I hadn't exactly been thinking that I didn't want to leave clues in case I got framed for a murder. But O'Hara knew why I'd been there. She couldn't possibly be dumb enough to think I'd murdered Bud and then pretended I'd stumbled across him. Then again, she did have a deep-seated vendetta against me.

Then there was Hightower's threat. Agnes Newman had seen Aunt Gladys with the brooms on the patio. Could that be twisted around somehow to implicate her in the murder? Probably not, but the one thing I knew was that the longer this case went unsolved, the more anxious Hightower was going to become, and the more she'd pressure O'Hara for a solution, and that couldn't be good for us. Not to mention the fact there could be an angry, unstable ghost roaming around who might harm someone else. I didn't want to be responsible for that. I had to try to get rid of it.

Jinx had scarfed down his food and was now sitting on the couch across from me, licking his paw and rubbing it behind his ear. "There are probably some clues to the killer in the barn. O'Hara wouldn't know a clue if she fell over it."

"I suppose we could go back over to the barn tomorrow. I have the ghost vanishing cream. If I rub that all over the barn, that might get rid of the ghost. If there even is a ghost. That still won't help O'Hara find the killer, but at least if there's a malicious ghost around and we can get rid of it, that's one less thing to worry about."

"'We'? What's this 'we' crap? I was talking about *you*. *You* can go look for clues. I'm going to be spending the day napping. I'm exhausted from tonight's activities."

CHAPTER SIX

The streets of Hallows Crossing were peaceful the next morning as I made my way to the brick mill building in which my office was located. Birds chirped, butterflies flittered, and puffy white clouds floated lazily in the cerulean blue sky above. One would never know a brutal murder had occurred the night before.

I was almost at my building when the peaceful scene was shattered by an ear-piercing shriek.

"Jane! Jane Gallows! Wait up!" I turned to see Connie Steele, the head—and only—reporter for the *Hallow Crossing Cackler* racing down the street toward me, waving her notebook over her head.

"Oh no. See you inside." Jinx made a beeline toward the entrance to the building.

"Jane, can you fill me in on the Bud Saunders murder? I heard you were involved."

Connie stood directly in front of me. She was only five foot four, so I towered over her by three inches. Her flaming-red hair was sticking out in all directions, as if she'd been running her hands through it all night long. Her wrinkled lips were pursed. Her beady eyes were eager for information.

"I wouldn't say I was *involved*."

She fished a pair of turquoise plastic readers out of her cleavage, slid them onto her nose, then squinted at her notes. "Well, the police report says you were discovered at the scene of the crime with the body."

"I wasn't *discovered* with the body. I had a meeting with Bud, so I was the one that found him, and I called it in."

She waved her hand in the air. "Minor details. I also heard there was some involvement with ghosts."

From the sounds of things and the look on her face, Connie was salivating to write a juicy article including murder, ghosts, and possibly me. Visions of Hightower going ballistic when she read such an article in the *Cackler* ran through my head. Even though the town thrived on its reputation of harboring witches, goblins, vampires, and ghosts,

Hightower would not be happy for the tourists to think a ghost was running around murdering people. She'd already made it clear that somehow she was blaming my family. I couldn't let that article be printed, so I reached into my bag for some chocolate.

"No. That's silly. There's no murdering ghost."

"Oh really? Lots of people have reported seeing the ghost out by Bud's." Connie leaned toward me and lowered her voice. "I've also heard whisperings that there is a serial killer on the loose."

"Serial killer? Only one person has died."

Connie shook her head. "Not people. Mice. Three mutilated mouse heads were found in town last night. It's the work of someone demonic, I tell you. And you know what they say. These types of unstable miscreants start with animals and escalate to humans. In fact, that would be good to put in my article."

I popped a piece of dark chocolate bark into my mouth. The silky texture and sweetly bitter flavor swirled on my tongue as I brought my mind into focus. While Connie rambled on about her article, I cast the fugget-about-it spell. Bingo! Judging by the way Connie's face went blank, I'd hit my target dead on center.

"Now what was I ..." Connie's brows mashed

together as she tried to remember what she'd been talking about.

"You were asking about Bud Saunders's obituary." No harm in steering her in another direction.

"That's right. Do you have any remembrances of him you want me to put in there?"

I shook my head. "I didn't really know Bud all that well."

Connie frowned. "Oh, that's odd. Somehow I thought you did." She tapped her head with the end of her pencil. "Oh well, must be getting forgetful. Never mind then. You have a nice day." She spun around and waddled off back toward the newspaper office.

I'd averted a crisis for the moment, but I knew my spell wouldn't last long. My magic was limited, and I couldn't cast spells with staying power like Tess and Liz could. Sooner or later, Connie was going to remember about the murderous ghost and the mouse serial killer and put it all in print.

All the more reason to figure out who done it and put the rumors to rest.

"Someone bump off your client already?" Moe

Sharp stood in the middle of my office, wearing a trench coat and a fedora. One thing about Moe, he was a snappy dresser. I wondered where he got his wardrobe. Did ghosts have closets?

"I suppose you could say that. How did you know?"

Moe pointed to the window, which was cracked open. He'd overheard my conversation with Connie.

Jinx let out a snore from his spot on the couch. How did he fall asleep so fast? The cat could go from wide awake to dreamland in five seconds. I wish I knew his secret.

"You think he chiseled someone?" Moe asked.

"Chiseled?"

"Yeah. You know. Conned. Swindled. Maybe he was into something and got chilled off because he crossed someone," Moe said.

I thought about that for a second. Bud hadn't seemed like the kind of guy that was swindling anyone. "I don't think so."

Moe tilted his head. "Well, how was he offed? Chopper squad?"

"Huh?" Moe often forgot that I didn't understand shamus-speak. Detective lingo had moved on since 1948, and communicating with him could be a bit challenging at times.

"Yeah, you know, a bunch of goons come in with guns and…" He mimed shooting up the place with a machine gun.

"No. People don't really do that these days."

"They don't? Shame. Used to be a great way to get rid of a lot of enemies at once," Moe said. "Well, was it a Harlem sunset?"

"Moe, could you use English? I don't know what these words mean."

Moe flapped his hands in exasperation. "Knife. Was he killed with a knife?"

"No."

"Okay, I give. How was the guy killed?"

"Pitchfork."

Moe let out a low whistle. "That's a new one on me. What a way to go." Moe hitched his hip onto the corner of the desk. "All right, so give me the deets."

I told him everything I knew about Bud's death. When I was done, he looked out the window for a few seconds and then turned to me. "You think it was about the cabbage?"

At my confused look, he added, "Money. The treasure. Do you think someone killed him for the treasure that is buried on that property?"

I'd almost forgotten about the treasure. "Tell me more about that."

Moe shrugged. "I don't know much. Back in my day, I remember some sort of incident when people came digging for that treasure on the Dunbuddy property. Seems there were a couple of people that didn't want each other getting it. Big shoot-out."

"A shoot-out? Maybe one of the victims is the ghost."

"Nah. They survived. Treasure was never found though."

"Do you think there's really a treasure buried there?"

"Heck if I know. Doesn't matter what I think though. If someone else thinks there's treasure there and Bud got in their way, it might have hastened his demise." Moe drew his hand horizontally across his neck to illustrate.

"What about the ghost? Did anyone see a ghost on the property back then?"

Moe shook his head. "Everyone said it was haunted by Mary the witch, but I don't recall anyone actually seeing her."

"Okay, well, where did the people think the treasure was buried? Near the barn?"

"Barn? There's no barn on that property."

Things had changed a lot in town since Moe had walked the streets.

"Well, there's one now. And that's where Bud was killed."

"Near as I remember, the treasure was supposed to be near a tall oak tree, but who even knows if that tree's still there?" Moe cast a wistful glance at the window. "If only I could leave this office, I might be able to show you."

I felt a pang of sympathy at the look of longing that passed over his face. For some reason, Moe was stuck in this office. It was as if there was an invisible force field at the door. He had tried to leave plenty of times, but whenever he got to the door it was as if he smacked into a wall. He hardly ever tried anymore.

"So you still gonna investigate?"

"Got nothing else to do."

Moe nodded in approval. "That's good. Private eye code of ethics: never leave a job half done."

Well, at least Moe approved.

He got up and started pacing the room. "Now, you gotta do some real old-fashioned gumshoe work. Work the streets. Talk to the neighbors. Look for clues. In my experience, there's always someone who saw something. And that dame outside the window here said people reported ghosts. Ghosts or not, find out exactly what they heard and saw. Maybe it wasn't a ghost at all."

I glanced at Jinx, still fast asleep on the couch. I wasn't gonna wake him, since he'd already said he wouldn't be coming. I slung my tote up on my shoulder and headed for the door.

Moe called after me, "Put the screws to them, Red. Don't leave no stone unturned."

CHAPTER SEVEN

No one was at Bud's, so I parked in the driveway and headed straight to the barn. The only evidence a murder had occurred was the yellow crime scene tape draped around the area where Bud's body had lain. The quiet stillness inside the barn was eerie. The boards creaking as I stepped on them made me jump. The smell of dry wood, old hay, and tangy copper churned my stomach.

I wondered if Bud's ghost would be here. He'd been murdered, and that was certainly unsettling. I focused myself on feeling the spirits that might be in the barn, the ghost vanishing cream in my hand, but nothing came. It was almost as if this whole ghost business was a fabrication.

If Bud hadn't been killed by a ghost, that meant

he'd been killed by a human, and humans left clues. I decided to look around outside first.

The knee-high grass tickled my bare calves below my denim capris as I walked the perimeter of the barn. Bud hadn't mowed out by the barn in a long time. In fact, it looked like he hadn't done much in the barn in ages. The inside indicated the same. No workshop, and he didn't have any farm animals, not even a barn cat. In fact, it looked like it had been empty for decades. But if that was the case, what had brought Bud out to the barn last night? From the way he'd acted in my office, I was pretty sure he wouldn't have gone out there looking for the ghost.

I slowly made my way around the barn, scanning the grass for clues. Around back, I noticed a path in the grass. It reminded me of the path that led from our house to Agnes Newman's house. Agnes had beaten down that path by coming over and spying on us time and time again. Had someone else beaten down a path to Bud's barn? And what was at the other end of it?

The path led to woods at the edge of the property. The woods were dense with leaves and foliage, and I couldn't see what was on the other side. Only one way to find out.

I followed the path.

Inside the woods, it was a little cooler and a little darker. The path was clearly evident, though, and I cautiously picked my way along it. Chipmunks scurried across the trail. A blue jay flew down from a tree across the path and landed on the other side with a raucous caw. As I got further in, I could see a clearing ahead. It looked as if there was a house up there.

Click!

I stopped in mid-step, my heart skidding against my rib cage.

"Put your hands up and turn around real slow."

I did as told, turning to face a man that looked to be about Bud's age. He had a crackly, weathered face and dark, suspicious eyes. The shotgun he was pointing at my chest gave me the impression he wasn't happy to see me.

"You're trespassing."

"Sorry. I'm a friend of Bud's, and I was just over at his barn."

The man scowled. "A friend of Bud's. I don't think I ever heard him mention any young redheaded friend."

"Oh, are you a friend of his too?" I asked.

The shotgun didn't waver. "Sort of. Live over there." He jerked his head in the direction of the clearing. Was this Bud's neighbor that my uncle had mentioned? The one he was having the feud with?

"Charlie Henderson?"

The suspicion in the man's eyes deepened. "How do you know my name?"

"Bud mentioned you," I lied. "I'm Jane Gallows."

Recognition flittered across the man's face, and he lowered the shotgun. "You mean you're related to Gladys and Wanda?"

I nodded, hoping his experiences with my aunts had been favorable ones. That wasn't always the case.

"Oh, well then." He lowered the barrel of the gun, and I started breathing normally again. "Thought you might be one of them treasure hunters."

"Treasure hunters?" So it really was true.

"Yeah. Didn't you hear the rumors? Treasure over on Bud's property."

Charlie started walking toward his house, and I followed even though he gave no indication he wanted me to.

"I'm sorry about your friend," I said. I was actually trying to feel him out. From what my aunts had said, Charlie and Bud had feuded. They weren't really friends. Why would Charlie lie about that?

"Thanks."

Charlie was a man of few words, but he wasn't denying that they had been friends.

"You still following me?" he asked without turning around.

"Well, yeah. No. I mean, I just want to give my condolences."

By now we had spilled out into his yard, and I could see he lived in a rickety old cabin with a big front porch loaded with junk. A table was set up in the yard, and it looked like he had some sort of project going on. I squinted to see what it was. A dollhouse?

"Okay. You've given your condolences. Now get lost."

But I didn't want to get lost. I wanted to find out more about Charlie's friendship with Bud and the supposed treasure. And my dad always said that one sure way to get people to open up was to talk about their hobbies. "Did you make that piece on the table over there?"

"Yeah. What of it?"

"Oh, nothing. I was just admiring it. It looks wonderful."

That softened him up. He led me over to the table. "Doc says it's good for me to work on these miniatures. Keeps the brain sharp. Keeps the dexterity in my hands." He wiggled his fingers. He had large hands. Just the right size to wield a pitchfork.

Now that I was closer, I could see that it wasn't actually a dollhouse. It was just one room, like a scene or vignette. I looked down on a perfectly scaled miniature living room with a sofa, a chair, a credenza, even a little tiny rug in the middle of it. One of the figures had fallen over.

"One of your little people fell over." I pointed.

He scowled at me. "What are you, daft? That didn't fall over. That's the murder victim."

"Murder victim?" My voice came out squeaky and tight because panic was squeezing my throat shut.

"Yeah. This ain't no dollhouse. This is a replica of one of Hallows Crossings' most interesting murders," he said proudly. "That's what I do. Murder scene replicas."

I stepped back a few paces.

"Oh, that's an unusual hobby." My desire to pump Charlie for information suddenly became much less important than my desire to not be the starring victim in his next replica.

"Yeah. Gonna have some on display down at the Hallows Crossing Historical Museum, seeing as some of the murders are historical. Oh, don't worry though, I'm not doing one of Bud's."

That was a relief. Then again, maybe he didn't need to do one because he'd actually been the one that murdered him.

"So I guess you must have visited him a lot." I turned to indicate the path worn through the woods.

"Not really."

"But you were friends."

"Yeah. Well, we were *sort of* friends. Known Bud since I was a kid. These properties have been owned by our families for a few generations, so we grew up next to each other. So did our daddies. And just like our daddies, Bud and I didn't always get along. Fact, we spent our whole lives going back and forth between being friends and enemies."

This was not comforting. What if this was one of the times Charlie and Bud were enemies? Maybe Charlie and Bud had had a falling out over the treasure. Oh, that reminded me…

"You said you thought I was a treasure hunter. Have there been a lot of people here looking for treasure?"

"Not a lot. But I seen a few of them over at Bud's property more than once. I thought you were one and was going to scare you off."

"So there really is a treasure buried over there."

Charlie laughed. "Ain't no treasure over there. Don't you think someone would have dug it up by now? But I saw over the internet that old rumor had resurfaced again, and then when I saw that crud-box-brown Dodge parked around here more than once, I figured the treasure hunters had come."

"Whose car is that?"

Charlie shrugged. "Got no idea. Some out-of-towner. That's why I figured it belonged to the treasure hunters."

"Really? Did you see the car there the night Bud died?"

Charlie screwed up his face. "I don't quite recall that, but I don't always notice everything from over here. Maybe you want to ask Minnie Wheeler and Sophie Liberty. They live in the house across from Bud. Those two ladies keep a pretty good eye on the neighborhood. Now if you don't mind, I'm going to get back to my little scene here."

Minnie and Sophie were friends of my great-aunts. I hadn't seen them since I was little, but I was pretty sure Minnie's house was the red Cape Cod across the street and down a ways from Bud's. As I approached the house, the two old-lady faces peering out from behind the drapes told me my guess was correct.

Minnie threw open the door and rushed out to greet me. Sophie followed close on her heels.

"Little Janie Gallows! How are you, dear? How lovely of you to come and visit."

They pulled me into the house past a plastic-covered floral sofa and into the dining room, where a long lace-cloth-covered dining table had been set for ten. I looked around for other guests, but only Minnie and Sophie were in residence. Maybe they were setting up for a party.

"If you're expecting guests, I don't want to bother you," I said.

"Oh, no bother, dear. We're not expecting anyone. Sit. Sit." Sophie pushed me down into a chair, and Minnie fluttered about the sideboard, pouring from a silver teapot into dainty chintz teacups and putting miniature cupcakes with tiny red plastic hearts sticking out of the top on a tray.

"To what do we owe this pleasure?" Sophie asked as Minnie put the tea and cupcakes on the table and then took a seat across from me next to Sophie.

"Well, I was working with Bud before he ..."

Minnie nodded solemnly, indicating that I didn't have to spell it out.

"Anyway, I was wondering if you saw anything unusual around here last night?"

Their eyes lit up.

"Of course we've been seeing unusual things for weeks," Sophie said. She leaned across the table conspiratorially. "We've been seeing spirits and ghosts."

"Really? How do you know they were spirits and ghosts?"

"Well, it's obvious. Not only did we see them, but we also heard them." Minnie took a pair of tiny silver tongs with clawlike ends and pinched a sugar cube from a silver sugar bowl. She poised it over my teacup, raising a brow in question. I nodded, and she let go, dropping it in with a tiny splash.

"What did you hear?" I asked.

"I heard it howling," Sophie said.

"And I saw ghostly lights on Bud's property," Minnie said.

"And there was all kinds of moaning and groaning coming from over there."

Minnie nodded. "And clanking."

"What kind of lights? Like car headlights?" I asked.

Minnie shook her head. "No. Not car headlights. Why would I think that was a ghost? I know what car headlights look like. This was just one light. A ghostly light."

Minnie pushed the cupcake tray toward me. No sense in being rude, so I grabbed one and undid the paper around the base. Chocolate with vanilla frosting. My favorite. But I had a hard time focusing on my taste buds, considering what Minnie and Sophie had just told me. If there really was a ghost on Bud's property, then maybe he really had been killed by it.

"And last night, remember we heard the most horrible banshee wailing," Minnie said.

"That's right." Sophie poured some milk into her tea. "I bet that was when the ghost killed Bud. And you know what, that killing must have satisfied it, because we never heard a peep afterwards."

I frowned. "Well, Bud was just killed last night, so it's kind of early to know if the ghost is going to keep quiet or not."

"I know, but usually we hear it until at least nine o'clock, but last night we heard the wail around eight-thirty, and then there was nothing." Both ladies nodded vigorously.

"How long have you been hearing these noises?" I asked.

Minnie pursed her lips. "Oh, about a couple of weeks now."

"Every night?"

"Yes, I think so. Not during the day, though, just at night," Sophie said.

"Charlie Henderson said he saw an old, beat-up brown Dodge near here. Did you guys happen to see that?"

Minnie glanced at Sophie, who shook her head. "No. Haven't seen it."

"Was any car here last night?"

Sophie shook her head again. "No. Definitely not. I would have seen a car, because I looked out the window when I heard that awful wailing. I remember seeing the ghost light though. But the brown car wasn't there."

Now I didn't know what to think. Was there actually a ghost? It certainly sounded like it. But had the ghost killed Bud, or had this mysterious treasure hunter killed him?

Minnie and Sophie had said the brown car wasn't there last night. That didn't necessarily prove anything though. If a treasure hunter was illegally digging stuff up on Bud's property, then he certainly wouldn't park right in front of the house. It made me wonder, how had Charlie seen the car? Or maybe Charlie hadn't seen it at all. Maybe Charlie knew there was a treasure hunter in town, and he was making it up to frame someone else for killing Bud.

"Such a terrible thing," Minnie said.

Sophie nodded. "Bud was such a nice man."

"Yes. Didn't deserve those awful children."

"What was wrong with his children?" I tried to remember if I knew Bud's kids. He was in his mid-seventies, and I vaguely remembered him having two sons that were about ten years older than me. That would put them in their mid-forties. I couldn't remember anything much about them.

Sophie's expression turned sour. "Ne'er-do-wells."

"Could barely even bother to pay Bud a visit."

"Never amounted to anything. Always after Bud's money."

I glanced across the street. Judging by the dilapidated farmhouse and rickety barn, Bud didn't have much money. One never knew with these old coots, though. Some of them liked to live like paupers, then when they died, you found out they had a million bucks stashed away.

"Now I suppose those kids inherit it. Probably sell it off, and we'll be living across the street from a Rite Aid," Minnie said.

"Oh no, Minnie, don't you remember? Bud said he was cutting them out of the will," Sophie added.

Whoa. Wait a minute. "Bud was cutting his kids out of the will? Did they know that?"

Sophie and Minnie exchanged a glance. "Who knows. He often said he was going to do it."

If Bud was threatening to cut his kids out of the will, then maybe one of them had killed him before he could make good on the threat. Moe would have been proud of the gumshoe work I was doing. I'd come here with only a ghost as a suspect, and now I had a full list.

"Were any of his kids here last night?" I asked.

"Nope. No one was here last night," Minnie said.

"Well, except for you," Sophie added.

Great. The busybodies that watched the house could peg me as the only person here near the time Bud was killed. Perfect. Well, me and the ghost, but I knew O'Hara wasn't going to be satisfied trying to arrest a ghost.

I guzzled the rest of my tea, smacked my lips, and patted them with a napkin. "Well, ladies. Thank you very much for the tea. Now I guess I'll leave you to your party."

They pushed up from their chairs, flanking me.

"Oh, it was lovely for you to come," Sophie said.

"Don't be a stranger," Minnie added.

"Come back any time," Sophie piped in as I pulled open the door, stepped out onto the front steps, and skedaddled down the walk.

"Tell your aunts we said hello," Minnie called after me.

I waved and then hurried over to Bud's property. I wanted the chance to check out his barn and try to conjure the ghost again. And look for another clue. Now that my list of suspects was growing, I had a sinking feeling that I had my work cut out for me.

CHAPTER EIGHT

Back in the unsettling silence of the barn, I looked for clues. Given what I'd heard from Minnie and Sophie, I was pretty sure there was also a ghost, but if it was here, it wasn't making its presence known to me.

I dropped my bag on the nearest bale of hay, pulled out the ghost vanishing cream, and opened it. Blech! The stench was almost unbearable. If that wouldn't get rid of a ghost, I didn't know what would. I made quick work of smearing it on the posts to the stalls and around the door, gagging the whole time.

After smearing the cream, I shuffled around in the hay, looking for clues. It was fairly obvious from the hay still strewn everywhere that O'Hara hadn't searched very hard. I still wasn't sure if Bud had been killed by a human or a ghost, but if it was a human, they might have dropped something. Could it have been Charlie? For all I knew, Charlie was back home right now, making a vignette of Bud's murder with every detail perfectly the way he remembered it being after spearing Bud with the pitchfork.

My thoughts turned to the treasure hunter. Was there really someone in town looking for treasure, or had Charlie made that up? If it were true, maybe he or she had come here, and Bud surprised them. Maybe the noises had been made by this treasure hunter all along. But Minnie and Sophie had heard clanking and groaning and seen lights, which couldn't be the treasure hunter since they would try to be more subtle. Which begged the question, why hadn't the ghost scared the treasure hunter away?

I made my way over to the spot where I'd found Bud's body. Of course, the body and the pitchfork were gone, and red stains on the ground were the only reminders.

As my eyes scanned the area, something small and red lodged under an old oak barrel caught my eye. I bent down to pick it up. It was only about a quarter inch long and just a sliver wide. It looked like some kind of plastic. Images of Charlie's murder vignettes bubbled up. This looked like it could be a teeny tiny flower petal or a piece that had broken off from a miniature piece of furniture.

Could this be from one of Charlie's miniatures? But if it was, what was it doing in Bud's barn? Charlie said he never came over here. I couldn't be sure it was a clue, though, since it might have been here before the murder.

While I was crouched down debating the validity of my new clue, I heard the crunch of tires outside the barn. Shoot! Someone else was here.

What should I do? I could cast a no-see-um spell. I had just raced over to where I had put my purse, reaching in for the chocolates, when the squeal of tires announced another car arriving.

Darn! That meant more than one person, and more than one person meant I'd have to double down on my spell.

Car doors slammed.

"What are you doing here?" A man's voice.

"Never mind that. What are *you* doing here?" Another man.

"I followed you. Didn't want you getting up to any shenanigans on my property."

"*Your* property? This is going to be *my* property."

Fighting over the property? Must be Bud's ne'er-do-well sons.

"Guys. Guys." This voice was female. "The trespasser. That's why we're here, remember? Let's get this over with. I have an appointment this afternoon, and I need to take the car."

Crap. There were three of them, and they were just outside the barn door, and a spell wasn't going to work. My spells weren't that strong. I didn't know if I'd be able to whammy all three of them with it, and what if it only took on one? Then two people would be able to see me, and one person wouldn't. That would be incredibly awkward.

I opted to use a more friendly approach and disarm them with congeniality.

I popped into the doorway of the barn.

"Oh, hi. You must be Bud's sons." I smiled charmingly. "I'm Jane Gallows."

The tall one studied me, suspicion darkening his eyes. "What are you doing here?"

This must be the older one. He was balding but beefy, with the look of an ex-jock who had gone a bit soft. His once-handsome looks were fading. The other brother was thinner, with longish hair. Both of them wore stained T-shirts. A glance at the driveway revealed two rusted-out beater cars beside my ancient El Camino, but neither of them was brown.

"Your dad asked me to look into a few things at

the property." I toned down my smile. "I'm so sorry for your loss."

The woman stepped forward. Like the men, she was in her mid-forties. She was still pretty in an overly-made-up, bleached-blonde way. "I'm Chastity. This is my husband Brent and my brother-in-law Steve."

We all shook hands, the men still radiating suspicion.

"Why are you here now though? My dad's dead."

"I know, but I figured the least I could do was carry through with what he wanted."

"What did he want?" Brent asked.

Hmm. Maybe I should have come up with a story before I had the bright idea of popping out and introducing myself. "Um ... Rats. He thought there were rats in the barn."

"Rats!" Chastity's hands flew up to the sides of her face, and she sidled away from the barn.

"Yeah, he wanted me to get rid of them." I looked at the guys, appealing to their greedy side. "Figured I'd still give it a try. It'll be hard to sell the property if there are rats in the barn."

Brent narrowed his eyes. "Did you find any?"

"I saw some evidence. I spread some rat repellent. You might notice it smells like rotten eggs. I don't know if that will get rid of them. I may have to come back." I wanted to keep my options open for future clue scouting.

"Well, I don't think it was a rat that killed Dad, unless it was you." Steve cast narrowed eyes at his brother.

"That's a nasty accusation," Brent said. "Why would I kill him?"

"Maybe you thought he was going to make good on his threat to cut you out of the will, and you wanted to get rid of him before he could do it," Steve said.

"He wasn't cutting me out. He was cutting *you* out!"

"Well, did he?" I cut in. So what Minnie and Sophie had said was true. Bud *was* cutting his kids out of the will. And judging by what I'd heard, that might be a motive for murder.

"What?" Brent looked at me.

"Cut you out of the will." Apparently he had a short attention span.

"We don't know yet," Chastity offered. "The reading is after the funeral on Friday."

"Well, someone killed him, and it wasn't no rat," Steve said.

"Maybe it was an accident," I said.

"Or someone who didn't like him." Chastity's gaze drifted off toward Charlie's place.

"You mean his neighbor, Charlie?" I asked. "I thought they were friends."

Chastity shrugged. "He was always messing around with Dad."

"Yeah, but that had been going on forever," Brent said.

"How would you know, Brent? You never paid attention to Dad. Chastity was nicer to him than you were."

"I heard Charlie might not have been the only one skulking around." Maybe one of them knew something about this treasure hunter.

"What do you mean?" Steve asked.

"Did your dad mention any trespassers? There's a rumor of a treasure being buried here."

Brent's eyes narrowed at Steve. "Is that why you're here, because of a treasure rumor?"

"No. Like I said, I followed you here. I didn't want you messing with the property," Steve said. "You never did say why *you* were here."

"None of your business. My buddy Hank drove by and said he saw someone lurking around the barn, so we came up to see what was going on."

"How do I know you weren't here trying to dig up a treasure?" Steve persisted.

"Do you guys think there is a treasure?" I asked.

Steve and Brent glanced at each other.

"I don't know. This is the first I've heard of it. But if there is a treasure, it's *mine*." Steve jabbed his index finger at his chest.

Brent stepped to within an inch of his brother, pulling himself up to full height. "No, dude. It's *mine*. I'm the older brother, and therefore I should inherit everything."

"Boys ... Boys ... " Chastity stepped between them, her palms on their chests, pushing them apart. "Stop this fighting. Your dad has barely been gone a day, and you're already fighting over a treasure that doesn't even exist."

Chastity turned to me and shook her head. "These guys. Always fighting. There's no treasure here. The property's barely worth fighting over."

Brent and Steve stepped apart, obviously steamed.

"Now you guys shake hands and make up. I need to get back home so I can take the car to my salon appointment. It's too far to take the scooter," Chastity said.

"Fine," Steve said. "You leave first."

Brent glared at him. "No, you leave first."

I edged toward my car. "Well, nice to meet you all. I gotta run."

I hopped into my car and drove off, leaving the two brothers glaring at each other and Chastity tapping her feet in the gravel. Judging by the murderous looks on their faces, I wouldn't be surprised if there was soon another death at the Saunders property.

It was almost noon by the time I got back to my office, and I spent the next couple hours doing some accounting work and filling Moe in about my morning. When I got to the part about Charlie's murder-scene vignettes, Moe perked up.

"That's wacky," he said.

"Yeah, tell me about it."

"Sign of a disturbed mind. Maybe he's the killer. Seems like it wouldn't be much of a step from crafting miniature murder scenes to actually creating a real-life one."

"I've moved him to the top of my suspect list."

Moe turned thoughtful. "I wouldn't discount those sons, though. Many a time I seen a guy get whacked by family members who wanted the money. We need to find out more about this will."

"Yeah, got that on my list." Did Moe think I was stupid? I knew how to do basic detective work.

"Right. You know what to do. Follow the clues."

Problem was I only had one clue.

Jinx snored on the couch the whole time we were talking, so I just left him there in the middle of the afternoon when I needed to get some fresh air and resupply my chocolate stash.

The ambiance inside Charming Chocolates was as delicious as usual. Joe's chocolatey gaze drew me to the counter like a moth to a flame.

"Jane, so good to see you." Joe's eyes twinkled. "What did you think of my special candy?"

"It was delicious." It *had* been delicious, with a unique twang to it. "What did you put in it?"

Joe smiled, revealing the dimple on his cheek. "That's my secret. I couldn't tell you, or I'd have to kill you. Now what can I get for you today?"

And just like that, he was all business. I ordered an assortment of caramels and left the shop.

As I was on my way back to my office, something

familiar inside the nail salon caught my eye. Aunt Gladys. What was she doing in there? She never got her nails done. Tess, who was seated beside her, looked up and caught my eye. She gestured for me to join them.

I opened the door, and much to my surprise, Chastity Saunders was on the other side.

Her brows rose, indicating she was as surprised to see me as I was to see her. This must have been the spa appointment she mentioned.

"Oh. Hi. Jane, right?" she said.

"Yes. Nice to see you."

Her gaze wavered uncertainly. "Did you come here looking for me?"

"Oh no. Just coincidence. My aunt is in here." I pointed to Aunt Gladys.

She looked back inside. "Oh, well. Nice running into you. Have a great day."

"You too." As she walked off, I wondered if I should call her back. When we had been at Bud's, Steve had said she paid more attention to Bud than Brent did. Maybe they were close. And she'd mentioned something about Charlie. Maybe Bud had told her something about him or she'd seen something. Given his creepy vignettes and the path between his house and Bud's that he denied making, I was almost certain Charlie was lying about something.

I continued inside the shop instead. If I was going to question her, I'd have to think carefully about how to word it.

I sat down beside Tess. Glad's hand was on the table. Lucy, the nail girl, was applying acrylic nails to the fingertips of one hand. Her nails on the other hand were all chipped and broken.

"Check out my nails." Aunt Gladys wiggled her fingers. "Tess is treating me to new nails. Mine are getting all broken and dirty what with my problems with the brooms and falling down in the dirt all the time."

Tess shot me a knowing look behind Glad's back. Apparently she'd noticed that Aunt Glad was more concerned about her predicament than she let on and had brought her here for a little pick-me-up.

"I'm surprised I've never done this before," Aunt Glad said. "This place is a hotbed of gossip. I found out that Heda James is having an affair, and murder victim Bud Saunders's daughter-in-law was sitting right there just a few minutes ago."

"Did she say anything about what happened to Bud?" I asked.

Lucy spoke up. "Nah. She seemed upset about it.

We know her pretty well. She comes in almost every day."

"Almost every day? Isn't that a lot for nails?" I looked down at my plain fingernails. I'd never considered getting my nails done before. In my line of work, it seemed impractical. I often found myself scratching around in old drawers, driveways, and even dumpsters for clues.

"It is, but she deserves to treat herself. Being married to that louse." Lucy stopped her work, her brown eyes looking up at us above the blue mask over her mouth as she leaned across the table and lowered her voice. "I heard he cheats on her."

I glanced out the window to see Brent Saunders's rusted-out car pulling away from the curb. Sympathy for Chastity bubbled up inside me. If it was all over the nail salon that her husband cheated on her, chances were Chastity probably knew about it. Poor thing, consoling herself with manicures and spa treatments. Why did she stay with him? Maybe she couldn't afford to leave, but if not, how did she afford spa treatments?

"Help me pick out a color, Jane." Aunt Gladys's voice drew me back to the present, and I looked at the bottles she was holding up. "Do you like the orange, the purple, or the blue?"

"Blue."

"Blue it is! And put some sparkles or something fancy on the tips." Gladys pushed the blue polish toward Lucy.

"It's good to see you so happy and chipper," I said.

"Yeah. I was getting a little bit down, but I feel much better today. Tess made a nice potion ... er ... soothing tea for me." Gladys winked.

I frowned at Tess. The last time she had made one of her potions, it had affected Aunt Gladys strangely, and she'd gone off the rails.

"Don't worry. It's very mild," Tess said.

Aunt Gladys did seem happier, and she wasn't doing anything wacky. Who was I to question Tess's witchcraft anyway? I couldn't even make potions.

"I see you went to our favorite chocolate store." Tess looked pointedly at the white bag sitting on the seat beside me and wiggled her perfectly plucked brows.

I passed around some of the chocolates. "You know I can't live without my chocolate."

"You sure it's not that hunky chocolate maker you go there for?" Aunt Glad said. "Hey, you want me to whammy him with a sex hex?"

Lucy stopped working on the nails and glanced

up at Gladys, her brows mashed together like battling caterpillars.

Glad glanced at her then must have realized she'd messed up and talked "witch talk" in front of a human. "I mean, do you want me to talk to him for you, dear? I could fix you up."

"No!" I didn't need any fixing up.

"It doesn't have to be anything permanent, you know, dear. Why, when I was younger, I had lots of boyfriends, and some of them only lasted one night."

Aunt Gladys talking about her sex life was my cue to leave.

"Thanks, but I've sworn off men for the moment."

I didn't have to be psychic to know it was a smart idea to get out of there before the two of them ganged up on me with this fixing-up business. "Well, I've got to get back to work. You guys have a nice time. Will I see you for dinner tonight?"

"Of course. Zelda's making lamb, and I wouldn't want to miss out on that. Besides, where else would we go?"

CHAPTER NINE

"I hope you're refreshed. You slept all day," I said to Jinx later that night as we walked up the steps of the mansion for dinner.

"I'm nocturnal."

"Speaking of which, I hope you aren't going to maim any mice tonight."

"Nah. I won't be hungry. We're having lamb for dinner, and that's my favorite."

We opened the front door to the mansion to find our housekeeper, Zelda, standing in the hallway. She was wearing an apron dotted with flying pigs and an angry expression on her face. She jabbed her index finger at Jinx.

"Choo!" she said. Her accent was always heavier when she was angry. She was angry a lot, and when she'd first started working for us, it had taken me a while to realize that "choo" meant "you."

"Choo to you too," Jinx said, except all Zelda heard was "Meow."

"Did choo leave a dead mouse outside the kitchen door?"

"Who, me? Nope. Must have been another cat. What about that pack of thirteen black cats in the barn?"

The thirteen cats had been known to chew a rodent or two, but I was sure the mouse had been from Jinx.

"Don't choo look at me with those fake-innocent eyes." Zelda scowled at Jinx for a few more seconds before turning her dark, smoldering eyes on me. "Your cat is problematic. Can't you do something about him?"

"Me? I have no control over that beast, trust me."

Zelda threw her hands up in disgust. "Choo people! Impossible!" She stomped off toward the kitchen, leaving me and Jinx looking at each other in the foyer.

"That was weird," Jinx said.

Actually it wasn't. Zelda was prone to irrational outbursts. But we didn't have much of a choice, as we'd been through dozens of housekeepers in the past several years. Zelda was the only one that had stuck.

I followed Jinx down the mahogany-paneled hallway, past the parade of dusty gilt-framed paintings of dead relatives, and into the dining room with its ginormous golden crystal chandelier.

The food was set out on a hunting board, a mammoth piece of furniture with three-dimensional carved deer and fanged boars on it. It looked like something one might've seen in King Arthur's castle, and I had been told it was practically old enough to have been there. Everyone was helping themselves. Aunt Glad was showing off her new nails.

"Jane! Can you believe I broke one already?" She showed me her pinky finger with part of the nail broken off. "I got overexcited about Tess's potion. Didn't help me a bit with the brooms, though. Must be too early for that." She let out a giant hiccup.

Tess turned from her spot at the buffet, looking at Aunt Glad with concerned eyes. "Auntie, you didn't drink too much of that potion, did you? Remember I told you only one thimbleful a day."

Aunt Glad looked shocked. "Of course not, my dear. I always do as told."

Tess's eyes met mine. Since when did Glad do as told? Maybe a potion wasn't a good idea after all.

"I don't think that Agnes Newman will be bothering us too much," Aunt Wanda said as we all took our seats.

"Who?" Hooter inched forward on his perch, looking at Wanda with giant owlish eyes.

She turned to him and raised her voice. "Agnes Newman."

"Why not?" Liz asked.

"I put a poison-ivy hex around the perimeter of the fence. Be careful if you go out there. I don't think Agnes is gonna have time to come spying on us. She'll be too busy scratching herself."

"So how is your case going, Jane? Did you find your ghost?" Uncle Cosmo glanced down the length of the table. "Lucretia, can you pass the salt?"

The long dining room table had been in the family for centuries and could seat twenty. Although we didn't have that many now, we often liked to spread out. Lucretia was at the head of the table opposite Uncle Cosmo. She took the crystal salt shaker, drew it back, and then zoomed it forward, letting go like a shuffleboard player going for the end zone. The conversation stopped as we watched it sail past each one of our plates. Uncle Cosmo caught it just before it tipped off his end of the table.

"Ten points for that one, Lu," he said. We kept

score about how far we could slide things down that table.

"I didn't find a ghost," I said. "I did talk to Minnie Wheeler and Sophie Liberty, though. They said to say hi to Wanda and Glad."

"Oh, I should've mentioned for you to go talk to them. They keep a keen eye on that neighborhood. Did they see anything at Bud's?" Wanda asked.

"Apparently they've seen and heard the ghost. They also don't like Bud's sons very much."

Uncle Cosmo nodded. "Bud and Claire had a hard time with them. He's been very lonely since Claire passed, and they barely bother with him."

I cut a small piece of lamb and smeared mint jelly on it then talked around my food. "There was some mention about him cutting his kids out of the will. Do you think one of them would've killed him because of that?"

"Bud?" Cosmo said. "Nah. He was always saying he was going to cut them out of the will. It doesn't make any sense. Why would they kill him *now*? They would have killed him long ago if they thought he was really going to do it."

Good question. If Bud always threatened to cut them out of the will, something must have changed for them to act on it now. Maybe that change was the treasure. They'd both said they didn't think there was any treasure there, but what if one of them was lying? What if they'd heard the rumor or seen the treasure hunters in town and wanted to cash in?

"I also met his neighbor, Charlie Henderson," I said.

"Who? Who?" Hooter demanded from his perch.

Wanda turned to him and yelled, "Charlie Henderson." She turned back to the table. "I think that bird is going deaf."

"Old Charlie! Isn't he a hoot?" Gladys asked.

More like a crackpot. "Yeah, I guess you could say that. Did you know about his weird hobby?"

"What hobby?" Uncle Harold asked.

"He makes miniature replicas of famous murders," I said.

"Oh my, that is odd." Aunt Lucretia flipped a small piece of lamb to Jinx, who let it fall to the floor. He inspected it from every angle then gave it a thorough sniffing before finally eating it. I wondered if he was as discriminating with mice.

"That's even weirder than Cousin Freddy's death mask hobby or Sally Overton's collection of rare spiders," Tess said.

"And how about Tommy Bartlett's casket car hobby?" Liz added.

"Charlie mentioned he has seen some treasure hunters digging around out at Bud's," I said.

"Did he mention the ghost?" Aunt Wanda asked. "If Minnie and Sophie heard a ghost, then Charlie must have. His house is right behind Bud's."

Charlie hadn't mentioned any ghost. His house was a little way away, but it hadn't taken me that long to walk there. Surely if the ghost was as loud as Minnie and Sophie had claimed, Charlie would have heard it. I turned to Liz. "Charlie said the treasure hunter had an old, beat-up brown Dodge. Is that one of the guys you mentioned before?"

"Yes, it is. There's only one guy now though. The other one said the place creeped him out, and he left town."

"Probably the ghost scared him," Aunt Glad said.

"Maybe. I guess the guy still here is harder to spook," Liz said. "He's staying out at the Coven Cavern if you want to question him."

The Coven Cavern was a one-star motel out on Route 6. Not one of the town's finer establishments. I added a visit to the motel to my mental to-do list.

"I don't know if you should be going out to a motel to talk to some guy that could be a murderer," Uncle Lou said as if reading my mind.

My heart warmed at his concern, and he had a

point. Maybe I shouldn't be going out to talk to a murderer. Then again, I could bring my chocolates and hopefully get myself out of any trouble with a slow-motion or invisibility spell. "Don't worry. I'll be careful."

"Do you think the ghost scared the other treasure hunter away and killed Bud?" Aunt Glad asked.

"The ghost might have scared him away, but I'm not so sure he killed Bud. That Charlie Henderson seems a little unhinged. He almost shot me in the woods, then he conveniently brought up this treasure guy almost as if he was trying to push the blame. Minnie and Sophie never saw any brown car at Bud's, though, and I don't know if they just didn't see it or if Charlie was lying. He could have known treasure hunters were in town."

"Well, I don't know Charlie that well," Aunt Gladys said. "There was just that one night ... and that was a long time ago. He did have some weird kinks, but he didn't strike me as the type that would be a liar." Hiccough!

Wanda looked at her. "I don't think we need to know any details, Glad."

"Either way, Jane, you better be careful," Cosmo said.

"And don't forget, you want to follow through on

all the suspects," Aunt Lucretia advised. She watched a lot of detective shows on the big-screen television out in the mausoleum, since she was pretty much stuck in there during daylight hours. "You know what they say: the one who did it is often the one you suspect the least."

I knew that better than anyone. I'd still check out the treasure hunter and see what he had to say. And I wasn't crossing Bud's sons off my list yet, either. But Charlie Henderson had already lied to me about a couple of things, and in my book that made him a very suspicious person of interest.

CHAPTER TEN

The next morning, I headed over to the Coven Cavern bright and early, thinking to snag the treasure hunter before he went out for the day.

Jinx was in the El Camino with me as it sputtered across town. Yes, the car was ancient, but I liked it. The cat looked at me cross-eyed when I turned right instead of left toward the office.

"Where are you going?" he demanded.

"Coven Cavern Motel. Going to talk to that treasure hunter."

Jinx made a face. "That place smells bad."

"Yeah, I know. Sometimes you have to do things that aren't particularly pleasant in the interest of the investigation."

"*I* don't have to. I'm not going in with you."

"Fine. I don't need you."

"Yes, you do." Jinx sounded indignant.

"Don't."

"I help sometimes."

"Not often." I pulled into the hotel parking lot, noting that a rusty brown Dodge was parked at the end of the lot. That must be the treasure hunter's car. Now I just had to figure out which room he was in.

You'd think I could use magic to figure that out, but I wouldn't. Didn't need to. I could employ good old-fashioned detective work instead. It was much more rewarding to do it that way.

I drove past the brown car, noticing the plates were from Pennsylvania. I parked and went to the office, where I chatted it up with the clerk. He was a not-very-bright high school part-timer, so I was able to distract him easily. While he was out back looking in the lost and found for the glove I claimed to have dropped in the parking lot, I snuck a peek at the sign-in register. There was only one person signed in from Pennsylvania, Dave Brown, and he was in Room 10.

If Dave Brown had any sense, he wasn't going to spill his guts to some random redhead that knocked on his door. Luckily, I had another trick up my sleeve.

He answered my knock dressed in jeans and a dark-gray T-shirt, his hair messy from sleep, a toothbrush hanging out of the side of his mouth. "Help you?"

I shoved my hand out. "Pamela Wesson. Hallows Crossing Treasure Hunters Local Chapter Number Two Three Five Nine. You Dave Brown?"

"Yeah." He stretched out the word, his eyes narrowing.

"Right. Heard you were here through the treasure hunter community. Just wanted to verify you're looking for the Dunbuddy treasure. Wouldn't want you to get in trouble for not having the right permits."

"Permits?"

"Yep, we issue permits here in this town. Surely the other treasure hunters mentioned it."

"What other treasure hunters? There was only one other guy here looking for that treasure, and he's gone now. Just where did you say you heard that I was here?"

I ignored his question and consulted my cell phone as if I had notes on it. "Looks like the other guy didn't get a permit either."

"Look. I'm not going to be doing any more treasure hunting, so I don't think I need to buy your permit."

"You're not? Did you already find the treasure?"

"I wish. It's not that. That place is weird. All kinds of spooky noises and weird stuff going on up there."

"Ghosts?"

"There's no such thing as ghosts, lady. The biggest problem is that it's hard to figure out where the treasure is. The treasure was buried in the 1600s, but all the original plot plans from that time are gone. A farmhouse was built there about a hundred and fifty years ago, but who knows if it's on the original site of the Dunbuddy house? The geographic clues are in relation to the house that was there in the 1600s. Only someone who knows the area would know where to look for this treasure. It's acres of land, and it's just not worth my time digging for a treasure that might not even exist. If anyone knows where the treasure is, they ain't talking. Even though there was plenty of people digging."

"Plenty of people?" I asked. "I thought you said it was just you and some other guy."

"Just me and one other guy from the treasure hunter community, or at least we were the only ones who owned up to it. I don't know who the other person was, but after Seth left last week, someone else was digging around up there. Anyway, I'm done with that place."

My gaze drifted past his shoulder into the room, where I saw a duffel bag on the orange-and-brown-flowered bedspread, clothes folded beside it. "You leaving town?"

"Yep. Like I said, I'm done digging around here."

"I don't suppose you heard the guy who owns that land was murdered."

"Yeah. I heard. Sheriff was by here yesterday. I didn't see anything, though, so I couldn't help her much."

So O'Hara had questioned him. That didn't mean much. He could've confessed, and she'd probably be too dumb to take it for what it was. "And she's letting you leave town?"

Dave laughed. "Of course. I didn't kill the guy. I wasn't even here that night. Sheriff checked out my alibi and everything. Not that I need to tell you about it."

"Right. Of course. And you're sure someone else was digging around up there?"

"Yep, just yesterday in fact. And since I'm not going to be hanging around, I won't need a permit. Maybe you can go bug this other person to buy one of your permits. Now if you'll excuse me, I got things to do."

Dave shut the door on me, and I went back to the car.

Jinx had been sleeping on the passenger seat. He woke when I started the engine, yawning and stretching out his front legs. "You're done in there? What did you find out?"

Just like Jinx to have me do all the dirty work and then want to share in the spoils. "The guy in there claims he couldn't have killed Bud. He wasn't in town."

"You going to check his alibi?"

"Apparently O'Hara already did." Problem was I didn't know what his alibi was or how I could check it. I wasn't friendly enough with O'Hara to ask. And employing magic to put a blabbermouth spell on her and get the information out of her was skating the line. I wasn't sure if I wanted to go there, though maybe it qualified as expediting the gathering of information I could already get on my own.

"I think you better check it. O'Hara doesn't know her tail from her dewclaw."

"Maybe. But that's not the most interesting thing I discovered."

"No?"

"No. The guy said someone else was digging up there. But if the other treasure hunter had already left town, then who else was digging up on Bud's property?"

The dumpy part of Hallows Crossing abutted the more affluent section, which meant I had to pass my ex's office on the way to mine.

I closed my eyes when I drove past, as was my custom. I didn't need to see his prestigious black-and-gold sign or the line of customers waiting for his services.

"Hey, looks like you put the louse out of business," Jinx said.

"What?" My eyes flew open and homed in on Mitch's office. The sign was gone.

Maybe he was just getting a new sign. But as I slowed and peered in, I could see boxes piled up inside. What was going on? Had Mitch really gone out of business?

I should've been overjoyed, but instead, a pang of sadness bubbled up inside me. That had been the office that Mitch and I had shared. The one we'd opened together back when things were good between us.

No! I didn't still have feelings for him. This was

just some sort of weird nostalgia messing with my head. I was glad he was out of business. Wasn't I?

But I didn't have time to dwell on it, because the next thing I saw was a large sign in the window of Kellerman's hardware store announcing they were out of brooms.

My anxiety ratcheted up a notch. Aunt Gladys hadn't made any progress in recapturing her broom-flying skills. She was going to have to renew her broom license soon. If she didn't get the license renewed, she'd have to go to rehab. And if she didn't start making headway soon, she'd get more and more desperate, and there was no telling what she'd do. I just hoped Tess's potion would work. Better than that, I hoped Glad could stop herself from guzzling down the whole thing at once in her eagerness to fix the matter.

I pulled up in front of the old brick mill building that housed my office. It wasn't as fancy as Mitch's building, but I kind of liked the old-school vibe, and even though the stairs creaked and the building didn't have air conditioning, it was all mine.

The *Hallow Crossing Cackler* was lying in front of my office door. Big, bold headlines announced that a ghost had murdered an old-time town resident. My anxiety ratcheted up even further. Vera Hightower was going to be all over that. I was surprised she wasn't standing right here in front of my office, trying to blame me or my aunt. At least Bud had been killed with a pitchfork and not a broom.

Inside the office, Moe lounged in the guest chair, his feet up on the desk, tossing cards into the trash barrel. Swoosh. Swoosh. Swoosh. They flew through the air, disappearing when they hit the rim of the barrel.

He looked at his watch. "I've been waiting. Where you been? Someone knocked on the door."

I glanced back at the solid oak door with its pane of smoked glass in the middle. "Who?"

"I have no idea. It's not like I can answer it. Maybe you missed a paying client. You might want to get here on time, Red."

It had probably been Connie dropping off the paper. It wasn't as if people were fighting each other off to employ my services. Then again, if Mitch had gone out of business, maybe client traffic was picking up.

"So where you been?" Moe repeated himself.

"We were out detecting," Jinx said, taking his usual spot on the couch.

I raised a brow at Jinx. "Well, one of us was."

"Yeah, I really wish you'd put more effort into this business, Jane," Jinx said. "I can't do everything by myself."

Moe put the cards in his pocket, slid his feet off the desk, and sat up straight in the chair. "So what did you find out?"

I told him about my visit to the motel and my talk with Dave Brown.

"Yeah, that's what I thought," Moe said. "When you mentioned a barn, I knew the property had been changed. That house can't be more than eighty years old. There was an old farm on the property before that, but they must've rebuilt. Too bad we can't look back and see what buildings were there in Mary Dunbuddy's day. That's impossible now."

"It is? Why?"

"Everything was burned up in the fire of '44."

"The fire of '44?" I hadn't heard about that.

"Yeah, the town hall burned down. Arson. You see, Two Fingers Marchiano was about to go to trial for shooting up the Langly brothers. Back then, the police station was in the same building as the town hall. They didn't have fancy computers and stuff." Moe gestured to the laptop sitting on the desk. "Anyway, Two Fingers figured the best way to get rid of all the evidence against him was to burn the police station down."

"Let me guess," I said. "All the property records at the town hall were lost in the fire, so no one knows what the property looked like before Bud's family built the farm."

Moe shrugged. "Well, almost nobody. Course, you know how those old-timers are. They pass down information from generation to generation. Someone familiar with the property who has been around for a while might have a better idea of where the treasure was rumored to be buried. Bud's own kin might know what the property looked like before they bought it. Might even have an old picture. One of those tintypes or something."

That made sense, though it didn't narrow down my suspect pool. It just solidified my suspicions.

"Dave Brown also told me he heard weird things out there. That's one of the other reasons he's leaving."

"The ghost? Did you ever get rid of that thing?"

"Haven't seen hide nor hair of it. Weird, because they usually like to make themselves known, and the neighbors said it made a ruckus."

"Maybe the ghost got what it wanted. Maybe

Bud's death was the thing that sent it back over to the other side. Who knows? But I know one thing."

"What's that?" I asked, half afraid to hear his answer.

"It wasn't no ghost that was digging up Bud's yard looking for the treasure."

CHAPTER ELEVEN

I wanted to see if I could locate the spot where people had been digging for the treasure, so I headed over to Bud's. If I could figure out where they'd been digging, I might find some clues as to *who* had been digging, and that might lead me to Bud's killer.

I hadn't forgotten about the little red clue I'd found inside the barn. Could the treasure be near the barn, or maybe even possibly under the floorboards inside it? I wasn't sure, but I thought that sometimes when people replaced an old structure, they built right next to it. Maybe the original barn had been next to the new one, and his family had built right over the treasure.

Back to the clue. I was pretty sure it was from one of Charlie's vignettes. Maybe I could sneak over to his land and see if I could find a piece missing out of one of them. Charlie had grown up on the abutting property. It had been in his family for generations. The treasure rumor and location might have been handed down by one of his ancestors. Maybe Charlie had been inside the barn looking, and Bud had caught him.

Not wanting to alert anyone to my presence and risk another altercation with Bud's sons, I parked in front of Minnie Wheeler's. This time Jinx had decided to come along with me. No sooner had we hopped out of the car when Minnie's door flew open.

"Jane! Coming to visit again so soon. How wonderful!" Minnie rushed out the door, Sophie behind her.

Minnie rushed over to me while Sophie fixated on Jinx. "What a cute kitty."

Jinx scowled up at her with his best Grumpy Cat face. "Cute, my hiney. I am not *cute*. I'm fierce."

"Would you like to come in for a treat?" Sophie asked the cat.

Jinx's demeanor did a complete one-eighty. His grumpy face softened, and he rushed over to her, rubbing against her ankles and purring.

"Can you stay for tea?" Minnie said as we followed Jinx and Sophie into the house.

"No. I'm sorry, but I can't. I just wanted to stop by and let you know that my aunts send their regards." *And have an excuse for parking in front of your house while I scour Bud's yard.*

"Oh, how wonderful. They're really lovely ladies." Minnie's forehead creased slightly. "Though I do recall they *are* a little quirky."

"Quirkiness is a family trait," I said.

I followed Minnie into the living room. I could see Sophie tossing treats to Jinx in the kitchen. I wasn't sure what the treats were, but they must have met with his approval, because he was scarfing them right down instead of subjecting them to his usual sniffing routine.

Meanwhile, the clock was ticking, but I didn't mind the slight delay in my plans. I had a question for Minnie.

"Did the ghost make its appearance again last night?" I asked.

Minnie looked thoughtful. Sophie came into the room, wiping her hands, Jinx at her side.

Minnie turned to her. "Did you hear the ghost last night?"

Sophie scrunched her face for a few seconds. "No, come to think of it, I didn't hear it at all."

"Did you see any lights?" I asked.

"No. Maybe Bud's ghost chased it away."

"You know, I'm surprised Bud's ghost doesn't take its place," Sophie said.

"Maybe they're battling it out over in the hereafter," Minnie suggested.

"Like a turf war," Sophie said.

"Well, I hope Bud wins."

"Yeah, and I hope he's not as loud as the last ghost."

I bid them good-bye and left them discussing the merits of Bud's ghost versus the old ghost then headed over to Bud's. My eyes scanned the large yard and acreage beyond for signs of digging.

"Where do you think that treasure would be?" I asked Jinx.

"Beats me. I'd bury it under a tree," Jinx said.

An old stone wall ran along the edge of Bud's property. Grass and shrubs had grown up in some spots, trees in others. One of them was a giant, gnarled oak. Moe had mentioned something about an oak tree and how he didn't know if the old trees would still be standing after all this time. That tree looked ancient.

"It might be over at—"

"Oh look. A squirrel!" Jinx ran off behind the barn, where I glimpsed the end of a bushy tail.

Apparently what I'd been about to say held less importance than a squirrel. I guessed I was on my own.

I headed over to the tree. Dropping my purse on top of the stone wall, I poked around at the base of the tree, brushing aside leaves and poking the ground with an old dried branch. I didn't find any signs of digging.

A stone wall would be a great place for burying treasure. You could even leave some sort of a clue as to where it was, guided by the shapes of the stones. But when had they started marking the boundaries with stone walls? Was it as far back as Mary Dunbuddy's time?

I stepped back from the wall to look at it from a distance, searching for any inconsistencies in the wall. Perhaps an unusual stone or one that seemed misplaced or jutted out. If I were burying a treasure, I'd want some kind of marker like that. I didn't see anything though. I turned to look at the rest of the property, shading my eyes from the sun as I scanned the landscape.

Jinx trotted up next to me. "Jane, you gotta see this."

I followed Jinx along the stone wall to where it

ran behind the barn. My heartbeat kicked up a notch when I saw evidence of digging.

"Someone was digging here!"

"No. That was me. I needed to bury the remains of that squirrel. But look what I dug up." Jinx skewered a wire with one of his razor-sharp claws. It looked like some sort of an electrical cord.

I crouched and pulled. The cord wasn't buried, just camouflaged. It came up easily when I tugged. I pulled a length of it up. It led directly to the path in the woods.

"Why would an electrical cord be coming from the middle of the woods?"

Jinx shrugged. "Maybe the treasure hunter was using power tools to dig up the treasure."

"But where does it plug in? There's nothing in that direction ... except Charlie Henderson's."

I followed the cord, pulling it from its hiding place beneath leaves and pine needles. It was actually several cords, each re-wired so that it plugged into the end of the other. It led me straight down the path toward Charlie's. I must have been so engrossed in my task that I didn't hear someone coming up beside me until...

Click.

The heart-stopping sound of a shotgun being cocked froze me in my tracks.

"Oh, crap," Jinx said as he backpedaled toward the barn. I guessed I was on my own again.

I cursed myself for not being more aware. A private investigator needs to have eyes in the back of her head so no one ever gets the jump on her. At least that was what Moe had told me. It was a good thing Moe couldn't leave the office, because if he could have seen me, he would have been very disappointed.

As I turned slowly, I briefly wondered if I would be joining Moe as a ghost in my own office.

"Trespassing again?"

As I looked into Charlie's dark eyes, visions of his murder vignettes danced through my head. Had he already made one featuring me lying here in the woods with my chest blown open by a shotgun? Even worse than letting him sneak up on me, I had left my purse on the stone wall when Jinx had interrupted me. I didn't have any chocolate available to cast a spell and get myself out of this.

I decided to take a confrontational tack. Maybe I could shame him into confessing and giving himself up. Okay, probably not. He'd already killed one person and wouldn't hesitate to kill me too, but I didn't have any better ideas. I wondered briefly what Moe would do. Maybe I should have listened to his lessons a little more carefully.

I held the cord up between us. "What's this? Electricity leading straight from your house to Bud's barn."

His eyes flicked from my hand to the barn. "What of it? This is my property. I can have electricity leading anywhere I want."

"Yeah, but it didn't stay on your property. It went right over the wall to Bud's."

Charlie scowled. "That portion of the land *is* my property. I own five feet past that stone wall there." He gestured with the barrel of the shotgun to the wall before swiveling it back to point at my chest. "What exactly are you doing here again? You're working for Bud's sons, aren't you?"

Out of the corner of my eye, I saw Jinx skulking along in the woods behind Charlie. Was he going behind him to make a sneak attack from behind? And here I'd thought he'd run off to save his own hide.

"Why would I be working for Bud's sons?"

"You know why. You're a private investigator. Land dispute." He jerked the gun in the direction of

Bud's property again. "Those kids want to sell off Bud's land to a big developer. But they need my portion over near the stone wall 'cause it gives them the amount of frontage necessary for the zoning laws. Maybe they sent you to try to figure out how to finagle it away from me. Well, I won't have it! All I wanted was peace and quiet out here."

"What makes you think that?"

"I saw Bernie Alcorn out there with his surveying equipment just last week."

Surveying equipment? Was someone surveying the land to try to figure out where the buildings had been in Mary Dunbuddy's time? Maybe someone had a lead on where the treasure was and needed equipment to pinpoint the exact location. Or maybe Bud or his kids did want to sell the land. A ghost would have put a crimp in Bud's plans to sell. Had that been the real reason behind hiring me?

"Is that why you killed Bud? Was he selling out?"

Charlie frowned. "Bud? No, he'd never sell."

Jinx had skulked up behind Charlie. I could see him contemplating his options. Just what was he planning?

"So why did you kill him? The treasure? The feud?"

Charlie lowered the gun, his face a mask of

confusion. "What are you talking about, girlie? I didn't kill Bud. Sure, we feuded, but we were friends underneath it all. I just wanted to scare those treasure hunters away."

"So you're saying you killed Bud by accident."

"No. I don't know what happened to Bud, but it sure wasn't anything I did. I wasn't even here that night."

I studied him. Given the sad look on his face and the fact that he didn't have the gun pointed at me anymore, my private investigator instincts told me Charlie was telling the truth.

Charlie sighed, his shoulders slumping. "Okay. I guess I might as well confess to the truth."

"*Heeya!*" Jinx launched himself at Charlie, hitting him straight in the chest and bouncing off. He fell to the ground, landing on his side, then jumped up and shook himself off. He arched his back and hissed at Charlie, who hadn't even been fazed by the attack.

Charlie jerked the gun toward Jinx. "Damn thing's rabid!"

"No!" I lurched forward, shoving the barrel away from Jinx. "That's my cat. He's just a little weird."

Jinx's gaze flicked between the two of us. "Weird? I was saving you."

"I don't think I need saving right now," I said.

Charlie looked at me. "Are you crazy? I could have shot you. Are you talking to that cat?"

"No. No." I needed to get him back to talking about himself, not me or my cat. While I appreciated Jinx's attempt to save me, he'd launched himself at Charlie at the exact wrong time, interrupting his big confession. "What was that you were about to confess?"

"I didn't like all the people coming here and digging things up. Sounds at night. Cars driving by. Bud was always in his place by eight p.m. sharp. He never stayed out late. No noises or car headlights, seeing as those kids never came to visit him except that daughter-in-law. But ever since this treasure rumor started circulating, they've been swarming here like flies. So I put a stop to it."

A sickening feeling came over me. "Put a stop to it" sounded so final. I thought again about his murder vignettes. What had Charlie done? And whatever it was, had it resulted in the accidental death of Bud? "How did you put a stop to it?"

"I rigged things up so it would seem like there was a ghost. Figured that would scare people away."

Wait a minute. "You mean the lights and sounds that everyone reported hearing was you?"

Charlie nodded and pointed to the electrical cord.

"That's why I had electricity out there. See, at night, I would sneak down and set up some ghostly glowing lights and speakers to try to scare them off."

It made sense. That's why Charlie's miniature clue was in the barn. That's why everyone thought there was a ghost. But it didn't explain how Bud had ended up on the wrong end of a pitchfork.

"Did you set stuff up inside the barn?"

"Inside the barn? No. That would have been trespassing. I stayed on my own land. I wouldn't do that to Bud. Like I said, after all the feuding, we were friends, and there's loyalty in that. Course, if I'd known all my setting this up might have gotten him killed, I never would have done it." Charlie's eyes misted. Either he was a very good actor or my instincts had been correct. He was telling the truth.

But what about that little bit of plastic I had found? I could have sworn it was from one of his vignettes. Maybe it had been on his clothing and had fallen off over by the stone wall, and someone else had tracked it into the barn on the bottom of their shoe. Possibly even Bud. Or his killer.

"So the noises that Minnie and Sophie heard. The clanking. The moaning. The loud banshee wailing. That was you?"

Charlie looked sheepish. "I didn't want to scare

Minnie and Sophie, but I kinda think they got a kick out of it. Gave them something to do. And I was careful only to run that tape before their bedtime so it wouldn't disturb their sleep. It wasn't that loud, anyway, just a little bit of moaning and clanking."

"Minnie said it was loud the night Bud died. She thought it was the ghost squealing that it had made a kill."

"Well, I didn't have anything that gives out a loud screeching. Minnie can be a little fanciful. Maybe she was exaggerating a bit. And besides, I wasn't home the night Bud died, so I didn't even set up my ghost stuff."

That was odd. "You weren't here that night at all?"

"Nope. Was out at the widow Perkins's. Oh, there was some moaning and groaning, but there wasn't any ghost, if you catch my drift." Charlie winked at me. He was downright jovial now. The man could change moods as quickly as my Aunt Gladys changed witch hats.

"Gross. I need to get the backs of my eyes bleached now," Jinx said. "I can't unsee the image of this old guy and the widow Perkins in my mind."

I agreed. I was trying to unsee it myself.

At my silence, Charlie added, "Go on and ask her.

I told Sheriff O'Hara the same thing, and it must have checked out, because she ain't been back to arrest me."

I thanked Charlie and left. Now that the truth was out, he seemed downright friendly toward me. But unfortunately, I had come away with more questions than answers.

I still wanted to verify Charlie's alibi, but if my instincts were correct and he was telling the truth, then there was no ghost and Charlie had an alibi. And if Dave Brown also had an alibi, that left only a few who could have done it—a member of Bud's family. The question was, which one?

CHAPTER TWELVE

"Sounds like everyone's got an alibi," Jinx said when we were back in the car, pulling away from Bud's.

"Yeah, but which one of them is lying?"

"You could try a tell-the-whole-truth spell."

No. I wouldn't do that. No matter how much I wanted to get to the bottom of this, casting a spell to get a suspect to tell the truth was against my principles. "That would be like cheating."

"Not really. You don't have the means that the police have to intimidate people to tell the truth or the methods to check their alibis."

That was true, but neither did Mitch, and he didn't need to depend on magic. I wasn't going to either. "No. I'm going out to the Coven Cavern to see if I can catch Dave Brown before he leaves town and find out exactly where he was the night Bud died and also verify some of the things that Charlie told me about how he was the one pretending to be the ghost to get rid of the treasure hunters."

"Suit yourself. You could speed things along if you cast a tell-the-whole-truth spell on them." Jinx curled into a ball, apparently disgusted with my decision. "I'm taking a catnap. Wake me when we get there."

I didn't make it to the Coven Cavern, though, because I spotted Dave's beat-up brown Dodge in front of the hardware store. I pulled to the curb and got out just as he was exiting the store with a handful of shovels.

"Oh, hi." I hoped my voice sounded casual, as if I had just run into him by accident.

"Hi. Just stocking up for my next treasure hunt."

"Oh, is there another treasure buried in town?"

"Nope. Heading out like I told you before. So don't even think about hitting me up to purchase a treasure permit."

"Where's this new one located?"

His eyes narrowed. "Are you trying to get the jump on me and beat me to the treasure location? I'm sure it's not within your permit jurisdiction."

I laughed. Hopefully my most charming and innocent laugh. "Oh no, just being conversational."

"Umm, yeah. Well, have a great day." He pushed past me and started putting the shovels into his trunk.

Movement on the other side of the street caught my eye. It was Agnes Newman running out of the pharmacy with a large bag. She was scratching vigorously in all kinds of unmentionable places as she made her way to her car. Aunt Wanda's spell must've worked.

Unfortunately, Agnes's car happened to be parked at the curb in front of Mitch's office, which drew my eye to something else I didn't want to see. Mitch. He was coming out the door with a big cardboard box. What was up with that? I doubted he was really going out of business. Maybe he'd found even more exclusive digs.

"Ahem." Jinx jerked his head toward Dave, who was shutting the trunk.

I walked closer to the car. "Hey, so I was wondering about the ghostly noises that you heard at the Dunbuddy place. Did they usually stop around nine p.m.?"

He stood there, his hands in his pockets, as he thought. "You know, now that you mention it, I think they did. They didn't go on all night, that's for sure. I only heard them the few times I came earlier. But usually I waited until midnight and never heard a peep."

He shrugged and started towards his driver's door. "What's that got to do with anything anyway?"

I started to panic. He was going to get away! "And the night that Bud was killed, where were you?"

I knew what I was asking Dave was important, but for some reason I couldn't keep my gaze away from the sidewalk, where Mitch was standing with the box. He wasn't alone anymore. Sheriff O'Hara was talking to him. She was all smiles. I didn't think I'd ever actually seen her smile before, and wait ... was she actually giggling?

"Ahem!" Jinx said, more loudly this time, yanking my attention back to Dave, who now had the driver's-side door open and was about to get into the car.

"Oh one more thing." I felt like Columbo during the big reveal. "You said you were out somewhere on the night Bud Saunders was killed. I forgot exactly where you said that was."

He looked at me over the roof of his car with narrowed eyes. "What business is it of yours?"

Maybe I should've thought of a reason to make it my business before I asked. "Oh, nothing. I was just curious."

"Well, you know what they say." His gaze dropped to Jinx and then flicked back up to me. "Curiosity killed the cat." Then he got into his car, started it, and drove off.

"See, you should've hit him with a tell-the-whole-truth spell like I said," Jinx said. "Now you've got bupkis."

My gaze jerked back to Mitch. He had that charming smile that had always made me do things against my better judgment on his face. He looked up, and our eyes met in a zing of lightning. Not the good kind of lightning though. The really bad, unwanted kind.

He waved. O'Hara noticed him waving and looked in my direction. Her smile snapped into a frown when she saw that it was me Mitch was waving at. She whirled around and headed toward me.

"Great, now you've done it. Here comes Sheriff Oh-Horror," Jinx said. "Hey, you know what? This could be good. I know you don't want to mess with the suspects, but what about the sheriff? If you hit her with a blabbermouth spell, she might spill out the alibis for Charlie and Dave so you could verify them. That wouldn't be against your high moral ethics, would it?"

Would it? Technically, that would be information

I could glean from the police files. Lots of private detectives had friends on the police force that would tell them these little details. Mitch had often used O'Hara for this very thing. She'd pretty much tell him anything. But she hated me and wouldn't even give me the time of day.

So in effect, Mitch had an advantage over me, and I could easily level the playing field with just one little spell. I reached into my bag and pulled out a piece of creamy milk chocolate. Blabbermouth spell it would be.

O'Hara stormed up. "Were you badgering a former suspect?" She jerked her head in the direction of Dave Brown's car, which was puttering down the street, backfiring as it went along.

"No, I was just chatting with him."

Her eyes narrowed. "I don't think so. I think you're digging into Bud Saunders's death. I could arrest you for obstructing justice."

"I haven't obstructed any justice, and I'm not digging into Bud's death." I crossed my fingers behind my back.

"Oh no? I got a complaint that you were lurking around over at his place." She folded her arms over her chest. "And why would you be going there unless you were going back to the scene of the crime? That's what the killer does to make sure there's no evidence."

"You can't seriously think I killed Bud." I popped the chocolate into my mouth and focused on the blabbermouth spell.

"I don't know what to think. All my suspects have alibis. For example, Charlie Henderson—you know he's a little kooky, right? In fact, he comes into the station all the time looking for pictures of old murders, and then I find out he's making little doll-houses out of them. How weird is that? So naturally I suspect him right off, but turns out he was with Melinda Perkins. Oh yeah, at first she didn't want to tell me. It's apparently supposed to be some big secret even though the whole town knows the two of them are knocking boots. I finally got it out of her with my superior investigative skills."

Apparently the blabbermouth spell had worked. I wanted to encourage her to keep talking, so I said, "Wow. That's really great detective work."

"Yeah. And that treasure hunter. Dave? He was a good lead. You know, he was digging around that property, and I figured maybe Bud caught him and then he had to kill Bud. But his alibi was ironclad." She pursed her lips in disappointment.

"Oh really? Where was he?"

"Turns out he was at a treasure hunters' meeting over in Keene with more than fifty witnesses."

"Oh, that's too bad. So who else do you suspect?"

"Well, I wouldn't put it past those sons of Bud's. Nasty bunch, the two of them. And the older one." She leaned closer to me and lowered her voice. "I hear he cheats on the wife. Cheating don't hold no muster with me. I don't think it's a big stretch to turn from cheating to murder. But he's also got an alibi, and the wife verifies it. And why would she do that if he wasn't home and could be the killer? Because in my book, that would be a great way to get rid of him. That leaves me with son number two. Steve. He says he was home alone. No way to verify that."

"That's interesting. You sure are doing a good job investigating." I almost choked on what was left of the chocolate getting the words out of my mouth.

"Yeah, so I have only one guy on my suspect list, and if that isn't bad enough, I'm being pressured to find the killer at every turn. And Connie keeps writing those damn articles, and those get Vera all worked up, then she complains to the mayor, who complains to me. You know it's not good for tourism to have a killer running around, not to mention I have to work all these extra hours, and ... "

Apparently the blabbermouth spell had worked too well. Now I couldn't shut her up. I stood there listening to her ramble on about all kinds of things I didn't want to know. Like how the department was cutting back and making her job harder. And how her bunions were killing her because she was on her feet for so many hours. And how Hightower was getting on her nerves about this case. But it was the last thing she said that caused a chill to dance up my spine. It was a warning.

"Yeah, and you better watch out for your aunt. Reports are she was down at the Witch's Brew Lounge drinking up a storm earlier today and acting crazy. You ask me, something is going on with her, and it ain't something good."

I went straight home after talking to O'Hara. It was almost suppertime anyway, but what she'd said about Aunt Gladys had me worried.

Hooter was sitting on a perch in the foyer. He flapped his wings and craned his neck toward me as I entered. "Who? Who? Who?"

"Well, if you must know, I'm here to see Aunt Gladys."

He swiveled his head and then jerked it in the direction of the stairs. Apparently, Aunt Gladys was upstairs. Maybe she wasn't feeling well after her afternoon at the Witch's Brew.

"Aunt Gladys is napping. We're in the kitchen." Tess's voice drifted down the hall, and I headed toward the kitchen.

Tess and Aunt Wanda were sitting at the scarred pine kitchen table, their hands wrapped around steaming mugs. A pile of fresh brooms lay on the patio outside.

"Someone said they saw Aunt Gladys down at the Witch's Brew Lounge. Is that true?"

They both rolled their eyes.

"Yes. Seems she got into the bubbly down there. You know how she can't hold her liquor," Wanda said.

Tess held up a large cobalt vial. "And she drank the entire bottle of potion I gave her."

Wanda sighed. "You know, I'm a little worried about Glad. She's been out there almost all day, every day, trying to control those brooms. She's tried all different styles, but the truth is it's not the broom that's the problem." Wanda tapped the side of her head. "It's up here."

"Has she made any progress?" I asked.

"Very little, I'm afraid. I honestly don't know what to do. If she doesn't pass the test, her license is going to get pulled. She'll go into a big funk."

Nobody wanted Gladys in a big funk. Normally she was happy and chipper, but when she was in a bad mood, the whole town needed to watch out. She'd cast spells right and left, turn people into toads, unleash the bats in the belfry. We had to make sure it didn't come to that. But what if Gladys's broom-flying days were over for good?

A strange swishing sound came from the hallway. I leaned back in my chair to look out in the direction of the noise. Zelda was shuffling down the hall, wearing what looked like giant yellow mops on her feet and muttering curses in a foreign language under her breath.

"Zelda, what are you doing?" Wanda asked.

Zelda scowled at us. "What does eet look like I'm doing? I'm cleaning ze floor."

"Is that some new method?" Tess asked. "It doesn't seem very efficient."

Zelda turned to us and smacked her hands onto her hips. "Choo got a better idea? The vacuum cleaner is still broken. What do choo expect me to do? With all the animals around here, this place gets filled up with bat fuzz, cat hair, and owl feathers. One has to do something to keep it clean."

"That vacuum belt hasn't come in yet?" Wanda asked.

"No. And every time I try it, the thing wails like a banshee."

Wails like a banshee... That reminded me of a little inconsistency in Charlie's story. Minnie and Sophie had heard a loud banshee wailing the night Bud had died, but Charlie had said he didn't have any wailing in his repertoire of ghost sounds, and he hadn't even been home that night to enact his fake ghost routine.

Dave Brown had said someone else had been digging on the property besides him and the other treasure hunter that had left town. Charlie had also said more than one person was after that treasure. Could there be another suspect we had yet to identify that was responsible for both the wailing and Bud's death?

CHAPTER THIRTEEN

The next morning, I got to the office bright and early. The mill building where my second-floor office was located wasn't exactly in the most prestigious part of town, and as such, it didn't have a lot of occupants. Clients were few and far between. Apparently, having your office in a seedy, abandoned mill building didn't exactly instill a feeling of confidence in clients.

As I opened the doorway to the stairs, I noticed a shiny new lockset on the door beside it that led to a big office suite just below me. Good, more tenants. Maybe business would pick up.

Moe was lying on the couch, his feet up on the armrest, his hands folded behind his head. He sat up when I came in.

Jinx trotted over to the couch, hopping up onto the portion that Moe's feet had just vacated.

"Hey, man, this couch is cold." He cast an angry look at Moe, who scowled right back at him.

"Live with it, buddy," Moe said.

Jinx made his Grumpy Cat face, turned his back end to face Moe, and then curled up in a ball and started snoring almost immediately.

"What gives, Red? You catch the killer yet?" Moe asked.

"Not quite yet. But I do have some more clues." I told him everything I'd learned since the last time we'd spoken, including Charlie's confession of how he had rigged up the speakers and lights to scare away treasure hunters. I told him about the alibis that Sheriff O'Hara had verified. And about the tiny inconsistency of the wailing ghost.

"So it was a fake ghost the whole time?" Moe asked.

"I think so. At least it seems that way. Dave Brown, Minnie, and Sophie never heard the ghost sounds after nine p.m., which agrees with what Charlie had said. Then there was the electrical cord to prove it. I don't know of any real ghost that stops wailing at nine," I said. "That explains why I never felt a ghostly spirit there."

Moe nodded. "So Bud was killed by a human."

"Looks that way, but which one? Only one person doesn't have an alibi, and that's his son Steve."

Moe started pacing the office. "Yeah, it's usually a family member, isn't it? But why would Steve kill him? Do you think he knew about the treasure? Do you think Bud caught him digging up the treasure and they fought and Steve killed him?"

"It's possible. It looked like Bud had been pushed and fell backward onto the pitchfork. I'm not sure the killer meant to kill him. They could have started pushing each other around and he fell back by accident. From all accounts, Bud and his sons didn't get along well. But I think it was mostly bluster on Bud's part. I think he was angry because they didn't pay enough attention to him."

"And there's always the other son. His alibi was corroborated by the wife, and who can ever trust spouses that corroborate each other's alibis?"

"Good point. Normally you can't. But in this case, I don't see why the wife would lie to cover up for him. He was cheating on her, and she knew about it. If she suspected he was the killer, wouldn't she want to rat him out so he would go to jail? Seems like she'd want revenge and to get rid of him."

"Why wouldn't she just leave him if she wanted to get rid of him?"

"I don't know. Maybe she doesn't have the money to do it. I don't think she works, and they've got nothing. They share one old beater car. They have to take turns to go to appointments." Though she did manage to pay for spa treatments and manicures.

"Maybe he has something on her, and he's forcing her to lie for him."

I hadn't thought about that.

"Wait. Did you say they had an old beater car? Maybe that's where your banshee wail came from. You know, I had a '41 Buick Super Sport Coupe with a belt that used to slip, and it wailed all the time."

"I think cars are made a little differently now, Moe." Did cars still have belts? My ancient El Camino had belts. Belts seemed like something even new cars would have, but Brent and Chastity's car was almost as old as mine.

What if Chastity had lied to cover for Brent, and the wailing sound really was from their car? I flipped open my laptop and did a quick search for their address. It wouldn't be too hard to figure out if the car made noises like that. I'd just go to their house and wait until one of them went out in the car then follow it to see if it made an awful wailing sound.

Moe was still pacing. "Looks like you've got to go back to the barn, Red. Now that you've eliminated some of the suspects, you might have a fresh eye for clues. Look in particular for anything that points to those sons."

I left Jinx on the couch and headed to the chocolate shop. I needed a chocolate fix, and the prospect of seeing Joe didn't hurt either. I didn't like the way my morning was going, so it would be a nice pick-me-up. But Joe wasn't in the shop. Instead, a perky young blonde eagerly helped me with my purchase of dark-chocolate peppermint bark.

As I got back into my car, I thought I heard a cackle split the air. My heart stilled. Was that Aunt Gladys? I held my breath, straining to hear, but no more cackling came.

Maybe it had been my imagination. I was overworked and underchocolated. I felt like the case was stalling out, and I was having to retrace my steps back to Bud's barn again, with slim prospects of finding anything new.

I sat in my car and ate half a pound of peppermint bark. I deserved it, because the morning really wasn't going my way. Funny thing though. I had a sneaking suspicion that the rest of the day wasn't going to be any better.

CHAPTER FOURTEEN

As I'd suspected, my day didn't improve once I got to Bud's. I parked a little way down the road so my car wouldn't be seen in his driveway and started near the house, skirting the granite foundation, looking for dig marks. I wasn't surprised when I didn't find anything though. If someone had been digging near Bud's house, he surely would have noticed.

Charlie had mentioned seeing Bernie Alcorn out on Bud's land with his surveying equipment. I figured Bernie must have been down back near the stone wall boundary in order for Charlie to notice from his place. I had thought the stone wall seemed like a good spot to bury the treasure, so I followed it. After about five minutes, I found fresh dig marks.

Someone had dug a hole about two feet wide and then filled it back in. Had they found the treasure? Dave Brown had bought new shovels from the hardware store on his way out of town. Was he really leaving, or had he just been switching to another hotel and pretending that he'd left?

His alibi had been verified by O'Hara, but that didn't mean he wasn't the one coming here looking for treasure, just that he wasn't the one who had killed Bud. He could still be coming back here to treasure hunt. Then again, so could the killer.

I tossed my bag down and started scanning the area, walking slowly in a grid pattern, searching for anything that might yield a clue as to the identity of the killer. I was on my hands and knees, scraping around in the crunchy dried leaves and pine needles, when I heard, "Put your hands up and turn around slow."

I was getting a little tired of hearing that line out here, but this time the voice wasn't Charlie's. It was Sheriff Bobby O'Hara's.

I put my hands up and scuttled around on my knees to face her. Brent and Chastity were with her. Over in the distance, I could see Steve jogging up the field. Great, the whole family was here.

"She keeps coming over here and digging. She mentioned something about a treasure to me. I think she thinks there's a treasure here, and she killed my dad to get it." Brent turned to O'Hara. "Wouldn't that be just like the killer to try to blame the death on me?"

O'Hara narrowed her beady eyes on me. Since I was still on my knees, I felt at a bit of a disadvantage with her towering over me.

"He has a point, Gallows. Why *do* you keep coming here?"

"I told you. Bud hired me, and I want to see the job through."

"Really? Doesn't seem like he'd be able to pay you for it."

"Some things are more important than money."

"Didn't you find her with my dad's body?" Brent asked.

"Yep."

"And she said she was trying to get rid of rats in the barn. If that's the truth, why is she digging way out here? I think she's lying."

My arms were starting to get tired. I glanced longingly toward my bag, which held a fresh supply of chocolates. I couldn't dig inside with my hands up in the air, but if I could, I could cast a forget-about-it spell or a momentary confusion spell and make my escape. Would that be cheating though?

Steve jogged up to the group. "What are you guys doing here? What's going on?" He eyed me suspiciously.

"We were driving by and saw her digging," Chastity said.

"Technically I wasn't digging. Someone else dug this hole. I was just searching for clues."

"Clues for what?" Steve asked.

"For who killed your father."

"Why would you be looking into that?" O'Hara asked, her gun still trained on me. "I thought you were looking for rats."

My arms were really starting to burn. "You can put the gun away. And can I put my hands down now?"

She looked uncertain but holstered the gun. "Don't try any funny stuff."

My arms fell to my sides, leading to instant relief in my shoulders. I didn't dare ask if I could stand. "I was just trying to see the case through. Now that the rats are gone from the barn, I figured I'd try to shed some light on what happened to Bud. I feel loyal to my clients."

O'Hara huffed. "Yeah, you're all about loyalty. Especially like when you stole my boyfriend in high school."

Brent, Steve, and Chastity all looked at her with confused faces.

After a second, Chastity said, "Are you going to arrest her?" I couldn't tell if she wanted O'Hara to arrest me or not.

"Arrest her?" Steve asked. "Do we need to go that far? I mean, she is annoying, but she hasn't really done anything." Steve earned some points with me on that one.

"Yes, she has. She's the one that killed Dad. She keeps coming back to the scene of the crime," Brent said. I wondered if he'd been talking to O'Hara too much. She'd said almost those same exact words earlier.

"Well, wait a minute, why would she kill Dad?" Steve asked. Then he turned to Brent. "You're the one who keeps coming back to the scene of the crime here."

"I did not come back here. I drove by and saw her here," Brent said.

I glanced at the driveway. My car was parked quite a way down the road. But I suppose he could have seen it out on the street and recognized it as mine. Or maybe he saw me in the field. Or maybe he really was coming back to the scene of the crime. But if he was, why would he bring Chastity? Were they in on it together? Was that why they were corroborating each other's alibis?

"Are you accusing me?" Brent asked Steve. "You're the one that doesn't have an alibi. Where were *you* that night?"

"I was home. Neighbors can verify they saw my car."

O'Hara glanced at Steve. "Well, actually, no one saw your car until after nine thirty."

Steve ignored her and turned to Brent. "Who can verify that you were home? I mean, besides Chastity. I heard maybe you were with a certain someone."

I glanced at Chastity. Her cheeks were bright red, and she was looking at the ground. O'Hara's eyes darted between Chastity and Brent, a slight crease on her brow. Perhaps Steve's words had made her doubt their corroborating alibis.

Which made me wonder. Could the killer have been Brent or Steve or maybe even Chastity? They were the only suspects I had left. Glancing out over the landscape, I could see their cars in the driveway. They both had old cars, which could have squeaky belts that might wail like a banshee.

I squinted up at O'Hara from where I was, still on my knees. "Can I go now?"

She didn't look like she wanted me to go. She glanced at Brent. "You gonna press charges?"

Brent appeared to think that over for a while then must have decided better of it. "No. Just make her get out of here, and make sure she never comes back."

Why was he so insistent I never come back? He seemed to be keeping a close eye on the property. Was he afraid I might find something that would incriminate him?

I didn't want to linger in case someone changed their mind. I jumped up, brushed the dirt off my knees, and grabbed my bag. The trip hadn't been a total bust. Now I was second-guessing Brent's and Chastity's alibis. Not to mention Steve's. He hadn't come home until nine thirty. What time exactly had Bud been killed? Was it before nine thirty?

I couldn't look into any of the alibis right now, but one thing I could do was figure out who had the car that made a noise like a wailing banshee.

I trotted to my car and pulled away, giving them a little wave as I passed the driveway. But I didn't go far. I pulled over in a dirt road about a quarter mile down the street and turned with my car facing out. I had a fifty-fifty chance that one of them would drive by in this direction. If they did, I could follow them and find out if their car squealed.

After a few minutes, a dirty white Oldsmobile drove by. Looked like I'd be following Steve.

CHAPTER FIFTEEN

I followed Steve all the way into town, but not one squeak came out of his car. He found a parking spot and got out. I drove as slowly as possible to see where he was going.

Surprise! It was Bernie Alcorn's surveying office.

Had Steve been surveying the land to sell it to a pharmacy? Charlie and Minnie had both mentioned they'd feared that might happen. Or did he have some sort of a lead on where the treasure might be buried? Someone had said that information was often handed down from generation to generation. His family had been on that property for quite a few generations. He might've heard rumors about where the old Dunbuddy house once stood.

But the nonsqueaking of the car was a fly in the ointment. I had hoped to use that to verify the killer.

Maybe this was better, since I was sure O'Hara wouldn't give any weight to Minnie and Sophie's report of wailing. Maybe I could convince O'Hara to look into Steve further by letting her know I'd seen him go into Bernie's. Then again, knowing how antagonistic she was toward me, she'd probably see that as me trying to frame him for a murder I'd committed.

Maybe Steve had gotten his car fixed? There was only one auto mechanic in town, Julian Crosby. We'd been friends since high school.

Julian answered on the fifth ring.

"Hey, Julian, how's it going?"

"Jane? Long time no hear. What's going on?" I could picture Julian, a big bear of a man, wiping his greasy fingers off on the red cloth that always hung out of the back pocket of his jeans, his face cracked in a friendly smile as he talked on the phone.

"Nothing much. I have a little favor to ask."

"Shoot."

"I was wondering if you've done any work on Steve Saunders's car lately?"

"Saunders ... Sanders ... Hold on." A series of muffled noises came through the phone as I heard him flipping through the notebook in which he penciled appointments. He came back to the phone. "Nope, no Saunders in here."

"Okay. Thanks. You keeping out of trouble?"

"You know it. How's your cousin Liz?" Julian had a little bit of a crush on Liz. Liz didn't return his feelings.

"Still single if you're asking." Liz was going to kill me, but I couldn't help myself. Besides, Julian was a nice guy, and I thought they'd be good together, even if she said he smelled like grease and looked like Bigfoot.

I hung up just as I pulled into one of the parking spots at the mill building. The office on the first floor was still shrouded in craft paper, but I didn't have time to try to peek through the edges, because no sooner had I taken a step toward the building when I heard heels click-clacking on the pavement behind me. I turned to see Connie Steele running up toward me, her hair practically glowing in the high noon sun.

"Jane? Bad break in that ghost story, huh? Can you believe Charlie Henderson was behind it? There's something not right about him, I tell you." Apparently word was out that the ghostly noises being heard up on Kenwick Road were all fake.

"I don't know. He seems like an okay guy," I said.

Despite the fact that Charlie kept holding me at gunpoint, I was kind of starting to warm to him.

Connie's brows mashed together. "*Okay?* Have you seen those creepy dollhouses he makes?"

"They're not dollhouses, they're vignettes."

"Vignette, chignette. Whatever they are, it's not normal. He has an obsession with murder." Connie leaned closer to me, her red hair glinting in the sunlight. "And I think he killed Bud."

I shook my head. "Don't think so. He has an alibi."

"Well, I think he killed somebody. Maybe the people in those vignettes."

"Sheriff O'Hara said he gets the information about old murders from the cops. He makes the vignettes from past cases." I doubted Charlie was killing people to make vignettes of their murders, but then again, one never knew.

I could see the wheels turning in Connie's head as she tapped a pink manicured index finger on her lips. "Sure. Some of them. But how do we know that all of them are from old murders? But that's a conversation for another time. I'm doing an article on the fake ghost thing. I was wondering if you have any insights for me. I heard you were the one that got him to confess."

"I don't really have anything to add. He was just faking that there was a ghost up there to keep people away."

"Keep them away from what?"

I shrugged. "Who knows. He's an old guy. You know how cantankerous they get." I didn't want to let on about the treasure. Connie was like a dog with a bone when she heard something that she thought would increase circulation of the paper. The last thing I needed was her writing an article on the old Dunbuddy treasure.

I decided to change the subject. "So Hightower must be happy that there's not a real murdering ghost." I hadn't seen hide nor hair of Hightower since the last time she'd accused me of being behind the murder. That was a good sign. Maybe now that the ghost rumor was squelched, Hightower would back off. I knew she couldn't seriously believe that I or my aunts would be behind murdering Bud. She was just used to accusing us of everything.

"Happy? I don't know about that. I guess she's glad there's no ghost. Ghosts are expected in this town, but not ghosts that kill people. Of course, if it wasn't a ghost, that means it was a person. People that kill people are just as bad."

She had a point. Hightower was never happy

anyway. The sooner I caught the real killer, the better.

I escaped Connie and headed upstairs to my office. Jinx was pacing back and forth just inside the door.

"Where have you been? I didn't have my lunch." Jinx trotted over to the stainless steel cat bowl I kept in the corner.

"I thought you were sleeping."

"Catnapping. I don't just lounge around all day. Gotta get up to eat. You know I'm a lean machine and need to eat at least six squares a day."

I threw some food into the bowl, and Moe materialized from the corner of the office.

"Okay, Red. Fill me in. Did you find any clues out at the barn?"

"Someone's been digging out there. But I don't know if it was Bud's killer or someone looking for the treasure. I did find out some interesting information on his kids."

Moe hitched his hip onto the corner of my desk. "Spill."

"It seems that his son Steve has been talking to Bernie Alcorn. He's the surveyor in town."

"Why is that suspicious?"

"Well, for one, Steve has no money to pay a surveyor. And for two, both Charlie and Minnie mentioned something about a pharmacy being built on Bud's land. They must've gotten that rumor from somewhere."

"So you think the kid was hedging his bets on his inheritance. Maybe he chilled off the old man to get the money early. If a corporation was sniffing around to buy that property, he would want to strike while the iron was hot and not wait for Bud to die off and leave it to him."

"Exactly. Or he could've had a lead on the location of the treasure. Maybe he found out it was between a tree and a stone wall, and he needed a surveyor to pinpoint the area. Someone's been digging there for a while with no luck. He might figure it was worth borrowing the money for Bernie to get the exact spot. The only fly in the ointment is that his car didn't squeal." I looked at Moe. "If a car had a loose belt or something that made it squeal, would that happen all the time, or would it go away?"

"It's not usually intermittent. Once a belt starts to go, it's always going to squeal."

I thought about the vacuum and Zelda with her mop shoes. If car belts were anything like vacuum belts, then Moe was right.

"Steve said Brent was lying about his alibi."

"Is that the one where the wife backed him up?

The one having the affair."

"Yeah. Steve alluded to the fact he might've been with his girlfriend, and Chastity looked really embarrassed. Maybe she knows he was with the girlfriend and is too mortified to admit that he wasn't there."

"Maybe. Or maybe she's in on it too. Maybe all three of them are in on it together."

"I doubt that. It didn't seem like the two sons got along. They kept accusing each other."

"Could it be an act?"

"Doubt it." They really seemed to have animosity toward each other.

"Sounds like you got more detecting to do. A good shamus never puts the finger on a suspect without ruling out all the other suspects without a doubt. You need to get to the bottom of it so you don't go around toting the wrong ringer."

"English, Moe, English."

"Toting the wrong ringer, you know, asking the wrong person."

"Oh, right." I sat down at my computer and looked up the address I'd searched for earlier. "I know that. That's why I'm going to stake out Brent and Chastity tonight to see if their car makes a squealing noise. If it does, then I know which suspects to focus on."

CHAPTER SIXTEEN

I figured suppertime would be a good time to stake out Brent and Chastity's place. Maybe one of them would go out after supper, or I could catch them coming home in the car. Did Brent even work? Either way, I figured if I headed out to their house around suppertime, at some point, the car would either be coming or going, and I could see if it squealed.

Jinx deigned to accompany me. An unwelcome sight met us in the parking lot. Vera Hightower. She was coming out of the mysterious office on the first floor. Oh, crap! Don't tell me that the office was hers.

Her face contorted into a scowl as soon as she saw me. "Jane. I want to talk to you."

"Is that your new office?" I asked.

She looked behind her. "No. I wouldn't be caught dead having an office in this sleazy mill. I was just delivering the new office welcome basket. All businesses get it. Never mind that. I want to talk to you about your aunt."

"What about my aunt?" Had she been caught at the Witch's Brew Lounge again? Was she flying brooms around the town square? I hoped Tess hadn't made her another potion. She'd guzzled down the first vial, and the effects of the magic were still in her system.

"She's down in the town common acting very strange. I have a good mind to call O'Hara and have her taken in. You know Bud Saunders was killed with a pitchfork, and what other implement is very close to a pitchfork?"

I had no idea where she was going with this. "I give up. What?"

"A broom. And your aunt has been obsessed with them."

Oh, that's where she was going. Not good. "Did you call O'Hara on her?"

"I should have, but I didn't."

That was odd. I'd figured Hightower would jump at the chance to have any of my family members taken down to the police station.

"Why?"

"Mitch talked me out of it."

It was my turn to scowl. "He did?" I couldn't imagine why Mitch would be nice to my family. We hadn't exactly parted on good terms.

"Yeah. But I'm having second thoughts."

A cackling sound sliced the air, and my heart skipped a beat.

"What was that?" Hightower asked.

"Sounded like a raven to me," I said. "Well, I better get going and check on my aunt."

"Yeah, you better."

Jinx and I hopped into the car and sped over to the town common. The common was a lush, grassy triangular area in the middle of a cluster of shops at the end of Main Street. Standing proudly in the center was a statue of Paul Revere on a horse. Except now the statue had something extra. Aunt Gladys was riding behind Paul.

"Giddy-up now!" Aunt Gladys dug her heels into the flanks, her red cowboy boots clacking on the metal. A crowd had gathered, and she waved at them. "Out of the way. Out of the way."

I pushed my way through the crowd. Unfortunately, Sheriff O'Hara had beat me there.

"You come down from that horse now, Mrs. Gallows." O'Hara had her hands on her hips and was scowling up at Aunt Gladys.

"What? No way. You Redcoats get out of the way." She waved at O'Hara as if to shoo her away. "I got me some tea I gotta dump in the harbor."

Oh, no. She thought she was on her way to the Boston Tea Party. This had happened once before, and it hadn't ended well. It must have been the residual effects of Tess's potion. Hopefully they would wear off soon.

"Yoo-hoo! Aunt Gladys!" I waved at her, and she looked down at me. "Get down from the horse now, Auntie."

"Hi, honey! You coming to the party? Bring some sugar and maybe some lemon." She dug her heels into the horse again.

"No. Aunt Gladys. The party is over." By about two hundred fifty years.

"Say what?" She leaned over closer to me, wobbling in the seat. The statue was probably slippery. I didn't want her to fall off and get hurt.

"Be careful, Aunt Glad!"

"You get down from there now," O'Hara said. "You could be arrested for vandalizing public property."

I glared at O'Hara. "You're gonna arrest her?"

"Did you say I need a rest?" Aunt Gladys leaned

precariously backward in the saddle. "I am a bit tired now that you—oops!"

I watched in horror as she slid backward off the end of the horse as if in slow motion. The crowd rushed forward, catching her and breaking her fall.

Aunt Gladys threw her hand up onto her forehead. "Why, thanks, everyone." She stood up, brushing off her long black broomstick skirt. "Now where's the tea?"

O'Hara stomped over.

"Okay. Okay. Break it up everybody. You." She pointed at Gladys. "You're obviously intoxicated and making a public nuisance of yourself."

I rushed over. "I'm sorry. Really, really sorry. I'll take her home and make sure she doesn't make a nuisance of herself anymore." I noticed some brooms lying around the statue. That didn't bode well. Then again, how had she gotten up onto the statue? It was quite tall. Maybe her broom-flying skills had improved after all.

O'Hara turned to me, her hands on her hips. "Oh, so you want to take your auntie home? You don't want me to bring her in to the station?"

My chest constricted at the glint of smug satisfaction in her eyes. "I'd really appreciate it."

"Oh, really?" She whipped the cuffs out and

slapped them on Gladys then started pulling her toward the police car. "Well then, how does it feel to want?"

"I know who's getting some mice on their front doorstep tonight," Jinx said as we pulled up in front of the police station.

I might have argued with him, but the thought of Bobby O'Hara stepping out in the morning to find several severed mice heads on her front step appealed to me.

"Sounds like a plan. You stay here in the car, and I'll see if I can get Aunt Gladys out."

"Will do," Jinx said quickly. A little too quickly if you ask me. I was suspicious, but he'd curled up in the passenger seat and was already asleep.

Inside the station, Aunt Gladys had sobered up. O'Hara had handed her off to one of the patrolmen, a wet-behind-the-ears kid named Jimmy Carruthers. Military-cut blond hair, bobbing Adam's apple. He seemed like a nice kid.

Gladys blushed when she saw me. "I'm sorry,

Janie. I don't know what happened. You know I drank all the po- ... I mean that smoothie that Tess gave me, and I guess it's still kicking around in my system." Hiccup.

"You're not really going to book her, are you?" I asked Jimmy.

"Yes, ma'am. Sheriff O'Hara told me to."

"On what charges?"

Jimmy looked sheepish. "Drunk and disorderly."

"You're going to give her a breathalyzer then, right?" I knew that was standard police protocol. And I also knew that Aunt Gladys would pass the breathalyzer. She didn't have alcohol in her system, and breathalyzers didn't trigger on potions.

I rummaged in my purse for some chocolate. If worse came to worst, I could zap him with a never-mind spell. I didn't really want to do that, though, because he might get in trouble with O'Hara later. Better to have him be forced to let her go because they had no legal reason to keep her when she passed the breathalyzer.

His cheeks turned red. "Oh yeah. That's right." He opened a filing cabinet and pulled out a little breathalyzer unit then administered it to Gladys, who, for once, was cooperative.

She blew, and he looked at the device. "Huh. It's

not registering anything."

He shook it then handed it back to her. "Can you try again?"

She blew again. Still nothing.

"Well, I don't know what is wrong with this." Jimmy looked around the room, calling out to a dark-haired officer near a Mr. Coffee machine that looked like it had been there since the 1980s. "Hey, Parker. Can you check this out? I have a drunk and disorderly here, but she blows zero on the breathalyzer."

Parker took the device and looked at it.

"Is it this redhead here?" He pointed to me. "They're usually trouble."

"No, this one." Jimmy pointed to Aunt Gladys.

Parker frowned. "You're arresting an old lady?"

Aunt Gladys pulled herself up to her full height. "Young man, I am not old. I'm wise."

Parker smiled at her. "I'm sure you are." He turned to Jimmy. "Let her go, Jimmy."

"But Sheriff O'Hara said..."

Parker pointed to the breathalyzer. "You can't arrest her if she's not drunk. Maybe she's just a little..." Parker made loopy circles on the side of his head, indicating he thought Gladys might be loony. "Can't arrest people for that."

"That's right," I said. "My aunt needs special

care. And our lawyer certainly wouldn't like it if she was arrested under false pretenses."

"I don't need special care," Gladys started but shut up quickly when I jabbed her in the ribs.

"Well, okay..." Jimmy's voice wavered uncertainly.

I grabbed my opportunity before O'Hara came in and made a fuss. "So, we're free to go?"

"I guess so." Jimmy sounded reluctant.

I didn't wait for him to change his mind. Aunt Gladys had already had the cuffs removed, so I pulled her out of the chair, and we started down the hallway. Much to my dismay, we ran into Jinx on the way.

"What are you doing here? I thought I told you to stay in the car," I whispered. The last thing I needed was to have to explain how my cat ended up in the police station. Which made me wonder, how *had* he actually gotten into the station? Last I knew, he couldn't open doors. But he was resourceful. He'd probably slipped in when someone else opened it.

"Well, you were in here so long, I thought you might need some help," he said.

"We don't need any help. Now, let's go ..." I didn't finish the sentence, because just then, I happened to glance into Sheriff O'Hara's office. She was seated at her desk. On the other side of the desk sat Brent Saunders and a blonde. Was that his girlfriend?

Apparently O'Hara wasn't as dumb as I'd thought. She'd picked up on what Steve had said out at Bud's property about Brent and figured out who the girlfriend was. Was she checking if he really had been with her the night Bud was killed?

"Darn. I wish I could hear what they were saying in there," I said.

"Oh, no problem, dear, let me just cast a walls-have-ears spell." Gladys raised her hand in the direction of the office.

"No!" I put my hand on her arm, pushing it down. "No spells. That would be cheating."

Jinx made a noise beside me. He rolled his eyes. "Okay, Miss Ethics, would it be cheating if a friend overheard what they were saying and told you?"

A lot of private investigators got police information from the cops they knew. If O'Hara had liked me, she might even tell me exactly what Brent and his girlfriend were saying. She'd certainly tell Mitch. So overhearing something or being told by the cops wouldn't be cheating.

"I suppose not."

"Fine." Jinx trotted over to the office, and I followed, making sure to stay out of O'Hara's line of vision.

Jinx put his ear to the wall. "Okay. She's asking

where they were the night of Bud's death. The girlfriend's saying they were together."

"Where?" I asked, scanning the hallway nervously to make sure no other cops walked by and noticed my cat with his ear to O'Hara's office wall. Luckily, it was a small town, and the rest of the cops, besides Jimmy and Parker, who were in the squad room, were out on calls.

"At her house."

"They could be lying."

Jinx looked at me funny. "That's exactly what O'Hara just said."

Jinx listened for a few seconds, his whiskers twitching. "Aha! They *were* lying. Now they are saying they were at the Bubbling Cauldron."

I knew the Cauldron well. It was a seedy little lounge on the end of town. Figures they would go there for their cheaters' clandestine meeting.

"O'Hara's calling to corroborate," Jinx said.

Huh. I guess she did know a little bit about police work.

"Bad news," Jinx said.

"What?"

"Alibi checks out. They were at the Bubbling Cauldron at eight p.m. when Bud was killed. They're not your killers."

Dang. Now what? That only left Steve. Steve had been at the surveyor's office. So he was definitely up to something. But how to convey that to O'Hara? Or should I confront Steve myself?

I turned to leave and then realized Aunt Glad wasn't beside me. I'd been so intent on Jinx overhearing the conversation that I hadn't been paying attention to her. I whirled around to see her disappear into a small room at the end of the hall.

I hustled down there, Jinx at my side. We opened the door to find a janitor's closet. Gladys was inside, eyeing the brooms. I pulled her out.

"Come on, Gladys. I think I better get you home and get Jinx out of here before O'Hara sees us and arrests us on some trumped-up charge of bringing animals into the police station."

I didn't need Moe to tell me that the next step was to question Steve and find out why he had been at Bernie Alcorn's office. But I couldn't do that with Aunt Gladys in tow. I had to get her home safe and sound before I did any more detecting.

CHAPTER SEVENTEEN

I knew Moe was waiting at the office for an update, but it was almost suppertime, and I wanted to talk to Steve as soon as possible. I didn't want to miss out on Wanda's famous Cornish game hens with pineapple ham stuffing, either, but I didn't have time to go both to Steve's and to the office. Moe would have to wait until either tomorrow morning or after supper.

It might have seemed a little crazy going to Steve's house now that he was my number-one suspect, but I didn't plan on confronting him. I just wanted to find out why he'd been meeting with Bernie. I was a little worried that everyone else appeared to have an alibi except Steve. His alibi was only from nine thirty on, but Jinx had overheard O'Hara say that Bud had been killed at eight.

I always operated on the premise that I caught more flies with honey than vinegar, so my plan was to play to his sense of camaraderie and pretend I was taking his side in the feud he obviously had going with his brother. If I acted as if I thought Brent was the killer, then I could gauge his reaction. If Steve was the killer, he'd gladly play along. If he wasn't, then maybe Brent really was the killer and Steve would give me some information I didn't already have.

But my main goal was to try to get a look at the plans or get him to tell me why he'd been meeting with Bernie. I wanted some proof that he was doing something concerning the land behind his father's back so I could tip off O'Hara. Hopefully her animosity toward me wouldn't prevent her from following through on information that might solve a murder.

I wasn't sure what Steve had been up to with Bernie, but several people had mentioned a big pharmacy wanting to buy the land, and Charlie had also said that the kids were trying to somehow claim the land on the other side of the stone wall that belonged to Charlie's property. Either way, Steve was up to something.

Steve lived in a shabby duplex, the cheap beige

vinyl siding scratched and smeared with dirt. I was in luck. His car was in the driveway. I headed toward the front door, weaving my way around abandoned kids' toys. Presumably the neighbors', since Steve had no kids. My hand slipped inside my purse, feeling for the security of the chocolates at the bottom.

If my theory was correct, it was possible Steve had already killed once. I didn't want to be his second victim.

Steve answered my knock, suspicion flooding his eyes as he recognized me. "Aren't you that lady that keeps showing up at my dad's?"

"Yes. Jane Gallows."

"Yeah, I remember. What do you want?"

"Look. I'm just trying to help your dad. I was wondering about your brother..." I let my voice trail off, testing him out to see if my suspicions that I might be able to create some kind of a solidarity between us would prove out.

He frowned. "What about my brother? Do you think he killed my dad?"

His interested tone suggested that he could get on board with that idea.

I shrugged. "Do you?"

He scrubbed his hands through his greasy hair. "Maybe. Do you have some proof?"

"Maybe. I figure you have some suspicions of your own?"

Steve looked conflicted. This wasn't really going the way I had anticipated. I'd figured he'd either throw me out or try to push me toward the conclusion that Brent had done it. But instead, he seemed genuinely upset at the thought that his brother had killed their father. Clearly he already had some suspicions, but if he was the killer, wouldn't he be delighted that I was trying to put the finger on his brother?

"Can I come in?" There was no way I was going to be able to ferret out the blueprints or plot survey standing outside on the doorstep.

He stepped back and opened the door wider to reveal faded shag carpeting and saggy plaid furniture. I stepped in. The place was small. The living room opened into a dining room on one end. Past the dining room, I could see a kitchen filled with chipped linoleum and cheap cabinets. That must have been where the smell of stale beer and old pizza was coming from.

Steve must've caught the look on my face. "It's not much, but it's home."

It looked as if Steve could use an influx of money.

Possibly from his father's estate. "Do you really think your dad left you out of the will?"

"What? Maybe. He was always saying he was going to." Steve's eyes narrowed. "And I wouldn't put it past Brent to try to talk Dad into including just him and leaving me out."

"Really? Would you guys stand to gain a lot of money?" If Steve thought Brent was trying to turn his father against him, maybe he'd gone over to talk to Bud about it. And if Bud had been poisoned by what Brent had told him, maybe they'd argued. And if they'd argued, maybe things had gotten heated and ended in murder.

"I don't know. Dad didn't have any savings or investments. I have no idea what the property is worth."

"What makes you think Brent was trying to get your dad to cut you out?"

"Well, he's pretty sleazy. Just ask his wife."

"Yeah, I heard he wasn't completely loyal. Poor thing."

"Yeah. She suffered a lot. But that's not really any of your business, is it?"

"No. But your father's death is my business, and I want to get to the bottom of it. I just want to do right by him." It wasn't a lie.

"Well, I don't know how I can help."

"No?" I asked. "I think you might know a little more about your father's property than you're letting on."

Steve tensed. "What are you talking about?"

"Just that maybe you might know the value of his property, and if you thought you would be cut out of the will, then you might've taken action."

He glanced nervously at the sideboard, and I noticed some rolled-up blueprints. Ha! That looked suspiciously like site work from Bernie Alcorn.

Steve's entire demeanor had changed. No longer was he acting friendly. He took a step toward me, and I backed up.

"I mean, I couldn't blame you for wanting to determine the exact boundaries of the lot," I said quickly. "Charlie Henderson mentioned some sort of dispute near the stone wall that abuts his property, and with your father gone and all, it's natural you'd want to know exactly where the boundaries are. I mean, I assume you'd be selling the property."

I didn't let on that I knew he'd been looking into the boundaries *before* his father died. I didn't want to tip him off to the fact that I suspected him.

He folded his arms over his chest, and the murderous look in his eyes made my heart pound.

"Honestly. I don't see how that's any of your business. Maybe you should go now."

My eyes darted to the sideboard. Not until I found out what was on those plans.

"I'm sorry if I made you defensive. It's quite reasonable that you might have hired a surveyor." I tried to keep my friendly we're-on-the-same-side act going.

"Who told you I hired a surveyor?"

I shrugged. "People saw him on your dad's land." I sidestepped toward the sideboard, one hand reaching into my bag for the chocolates. Would it be cheating to cast a distraction spell so he didn't notice me looking at the blueprints? It probably would. I had vowed only to cast spells in order to get myself out of trouble if I was faced with bodily harm, which, judging by the look on Steve's face, might happen sooner rather than later.

Steve stepped between me and the sideboard. "That's none of your business. I'm going to have to ask you to leave now."

I probably should have left. Steve was obviously guilty of something despite the way he'd acted friendly to me earlier and seemed truly upset about his father's death. Maybe he was unhinged, with multiple personalities or something. But I couldn't stop myself.

I darted around him and grabbed the plans while at the same time reaching into my purse for the chocolate. I could zap him with a slow-down-time spell or a confusion spell and get the heck out of there.

I held the plans up in front of me and popped a sea-salted caramel into my mouth. "I think this proves that you're lying. And why would you be lying if you weren't the killer?"

Oops, maybe I shouldn't have accused him of being the killer.

"What are you talking about? I'm not the killer."

"Then why do you have these?" I shook the plans open, letting them unroll in front of me. "Aha! See you *are* having your dad's land surveyed so that you could sell out to a pharmacy." I slapped the plans down on the coffee table, jabbing my index finger toward the middle of them, where the drawing of the building and how it would be sited on the lot was. Or should have been…

Whoa. Wait a minute. "These aren't plans for a pharmacy."

Steve looked at me funny. "No kidding. They're plans for a conservation trust."

"A conservation trust? But I don't understand."

"Well, if you must know, I was having the land surveyed for exact boundaries so it could be put in a conservation trust. My dad had talked many times about how he wanted the land to be preserved. He didn't want a strip mall coming in and building on it or anything like that. And since we've been on the outs recently, I wanted to do something to prove to my dad that I really cared about him and our family home."

"I don't understand. You were going to have your land put in conservation?"

"A trust. He could live there as long as he was alive, but then after that, no one could build anything on it. It would go to the town. It was kind of like a gift to him." Steve's face crumpled, his eyes misting. "But then before I could even give it to him, someone killed him."

I studied the drawings further. It was clear this was no land-development blueprint. And it was even time-stamped eight p.m. on the bottom right, with both Steve's and Alcorn's signatures below. I looked up at Steve. "You were at Bernie Alcorn's the night your father died, weren't you?"

"Yes."

"But why didn't you tell that to O'Hara? This is

time-stamped with original signatures. It gives you an alibi for his time of death."

"Well, first of all, I didn't think I was a suspect, and second of all, I didn't want my sketchy brother to find out. This was between me and Dad and had nothing to do with Brent. I figured if he found out I had this conservation thing in the works, he'd do whatever he could to mess with it. I know he's after Dad's money. He wants to sell the land out to a developer or something. I wouldn't put it past him to bribe some town official to put the kibosh on the trust. Wouldn't be the first time he bribed someone. And I still want to go through with this to honor my father even though he's gone now."

Well, this was just dandy. Unless Steve was one heck of a liar and had some nefarious reason to want to turn his ancestral home into conservation land, he wasn't the killer. Plus the proof of his alibi was right here on the blueprints.

I left Steve's more confused than when I had gotten there. Steve had a solid alibi, so he wasn't the killer. But then, everyone else also had a solid alibi. Which meant that one of them was lying.

CHAPTER EIGHTEEN

"Where have you been?" Jinx's voice assaulted me as soon as I entered the foyer of the mansion. I turned to see him perched on a high pedestal, his tail curled around the neck of a bust of some long-dead ancestor.

"Investigating the case."

"Why didn't you let me know?"

"You were asleep. I didn't want to wake you up. You get grouchy when I do that."

"Me? Grouchy? You must be confusing me with someone else. You should give me a heads-up the next time you decide to investigate. Things might be starting to get dangerous now that you're homing in on the killer." He hopped down from the pedestal, his paws making a soft landing on the marble floor.

"I didn't realize you cared." Really I hadn't. He

acted as if all he cared about was sleeping and eating. Could it be that Jinx really had a heart under all that black and white fur?

A muffled bellowing sounded from somewhere deep in the bowels of the house. "What was that?"

"That's just Hooter," Aunt Wanda called from the kitchen. "I had to put him in the attic because we're having Cornish game hens. You know how he gets when we eat poultry."

The last time we'd had chicken, Hooter had gotten pretty upset and dive-bombed us at the table. No one wanted a repeat of that. His beak and claws were pretty sharp.

"Good. Maybe he'll eat some of those bats," Jinx said. Jinx hated the bats, mostly because he could never catch them.

The kitchen was spiced with the sweet smell of pineapple and ham mingled with the savory scent of roasted chicken. Aunt Wanda was popping some rolls into the oven.

"Where's Zelda?" Usually Zelda helped Wanda out or cooked the meals herself when Wanda wasn't in the mood.

"Night off. Supper's almost ready. Why don't you go out and see if you can get Gladys to come in." Wanda nodded toward the pool area, where Aunt

Gladys was seated at the glass patio table, an array of brooms lying on the pebble-textured cement in front of her.

"Oh no. Things still aren't going well?" I asked.

"'Fraid not."

I pushed through the screen door onto the patio. It was dusk, and the sky was painted in soft pinks and blues. The brightest stars were just starting to become visible against the darkening sky. Cicadas buzzed, and the lazy sound of the pool lapping at the edges added to the tranquil setting. The air was heavy with a hint of chlorine and the sweet smell of honeysuckle.

I sat down next to my aunt. "How are you doing?"

"Much better than last time you saw me down at the police station." Aunt Gladys managed to look embarrassed, though I knew not too much embarrassed her.

"Don't worry about that. It could happen to anyone who overimbibed potions."

"Too bad it didn't have the result I wanted." Glad gestured toward the brooms.

"Don't worry, Auntie. You'll get your vroom back."

Glad turned sad eyes on me. "But what if I don't? What if all I can do is this?" She flung her hands out toward one of the brooms—an older version with a wooden handle and straw for the brush end. It wiggled. It waggled. The brush end picked up a half-inch, then it settled back down with a soft "plop."

"That's great! You couldn't even move the broom last time." I added a measure of extra-enthusiastic encouragement to my voice.

Aunt Gladys made a sour face. "Well maybe I've made a little progress, but it's too little too late. You can't ride a broom that stays on the ground. Old Coven Days is next week, and I'm afraid I won't be able to fly in the parade. Not to mention my looming license renewal."

Old Coven Days was kind of like Old Home Days for witches. Our entire coven got together during the last August moon for a big party that usually lasted from ten till the wee hours of the morning. Aunt Gladys always rode in the parade. My heart twisted at the despondent look on her face. I put my hand over hers.

"Is that what you're worried about?" I asked. "It's not such a big deal. I've never flown in the parade, and I still enjoy Old Coven Days."

"Oh, Jane, you must think I'm a real complainer. With everything you've had to deal with given your limited powers. You've done so well without being a full witch."

I knew she meant it as a compliment, but to tell the truth, her words kind of stung a little. It wasn't easy growing up in a family of superwitches that had full powers when all you could do was cast minimal spells that barely lasted five minutes, and only under the influence of chocolate.

Aunt Glad must have seen the look on my face. Her expression softened, and she patted my hand. "Don't worry about me, Jane, I'll be fine." She held her hand up and wiggled her fingers in front of my face, showing off her sparkly blue nail polish. "One consolation is that Tess is making sure my nails are in tiptop shape. We're going to the nail salon again tomorrow. You want to come? You've been so busy with Bud Saunders' case that you haven't done much with the family."

A pang of guilt seized me. She was right. Normally our family was close. I did things with Tess and Liz all the time. But this past week, I'd been wrapped up in the case. It wasn't worth missing out on family time. "I'd love to go. Now what do you say we go in and have dinner?"

"I say that is a great idea."

In the dining room, everyone was already serving

themselves. We loaded up our plates and took our places at the table.

Aunt Lucretia yawned. "Sorry. I had quite a restless night. Still just waking up." Sometimes it was hard to remember that Lucretia and Henry woke up at dinnertime and slept all day.

"I was just telling Jane how much we miss her being around. She's been so busy with that Bud Saunders case," Gladys said.

"Yeah, cuz," Tess said. "I kinda miss you coming around the shop. I'm scheduling a nail glam day tomorrow with Aunt Gladys. You want to come?"

"Yep. Gladys already asked."

"Oh, good," Liz piped in. "I might be adventurous and go for pink nails this time." The table erupted in laughter. Liz was not known for being adventurous. If anything, she was super conservative. Her favorite nail color choice was usually clear.

"So anyway, how is that Bud Saunders case going?" Uncle Cosmo ripped the leg off his game hen with gusto.

"Dead ends everywhere, I'm afraid. All my suspects have alibis."

"Even that Charlie Henderson?" Aunt Wanda's eyes cut to Gladys.

"Yeah. He was with Melinda Perkins, believe it or not."

Aunt Gladys frowned. "Melinda Perkins? That tramp."

"Are you jealous?" Lucretia asked. "I think you'd do well to stay away from that Charlie Henderson. He has some weird habits."

Aunt Gladys smirked. "Don't I know it."

"No. Not that kind. I heard through the night-owl grapevine that there was something fishy about those creepy vignettes that he makes. One of them depicted an old cold case where they never solved the crime." Lucretia picked up the hen and bit its wing off then continued. "I heard Sheriff O'Hara was looking into it because something in that vignette was never released to the public. It was only in the classified police files, so it was something only the killer would've known about."

"O'Hara said Charlie got old files from the police station on the murders," I said. "He probably found out that way."

Lucretia shook her head. "Not from what I heard. This detail wasn't in the regular files."

Images of the red plastic piece I'd found in Bud's barn bubbled up. I'd written it off as something Charlie had left when he was setting up the fake ghost noises. But what if it wasn't? What if Charlie really was the killer? Steve had been surveying the land, and maybe that made Charlie nervous. He wouldn't have known it was to be put in conservation and probably just assumed the kids were going to sell it to a pharmacy or mall as the rumors suggested.

"But Melinda Perkins said she was with Charlie when Bud was killed."

Gladys shrugged. "Wouldn't be the first time someone lied for their lover."

I thought about Brent and Chastity. Chastity had lied for Brent, though I still wondered what her motivation was. Was she still so in love with him that she would've lied to protect him even though he was cheating on her? And what about Brent's girlfriend—would she have lied too?

Maybe I really wasn't as out of leads as I thought.

We finished eating, and Aunt Wanda surprised us with crème brûlée for dessert. As I was shoveling in the last bite, I realized I might have one more midnight detecting job to go on.

Liz's phone chimed, and she pulled it out of her pocket. "Sorry. I thought I turned this off." She looked down at the display, her brows mashing angrily together. "This is a text from Julian Crosby."

I choked on my crème brûlée, and her eyes

snapped in my direction. "Jane? Did you have something to do with this?"

"Who, me? No." I tossed my napkin onto the table and pretended to look at the watch I never wore. "Well, look at the time! I gotta go!"

I pushed away from the table and hightailed it out of there with Liz yelling after me, "Jane Gallows, I'm gonna get back at you for this!"

I rushed back to my office, delaying only long enough to inform Jinx of my intentions. Much to my surprise, he roused himself from his nap and trotted to the car with me.

"That old mill building has big, juicy mice that come out at night," Jinx said. That explained why he wanted to come with me. And here I'd thought he was trying to make sure I stayed out of harm's way.

The news about Charlie Henderson had me in a tizzy. I'd discounted that little piece of plastic I'd found near Bud's body, thinking that Charlie had probably dropped it there when he was setting up his fake ghost speaker. But what if he had really dropped it when he was murdering Bud? What if somehow he'd gotten Melinda Perkins to lie for him? But that begged the question: what was his motivation to murder Bud?

"Liars and cheats. That's what murderers are," Moe said after I had filled him in on everything I'd learned since we'd last talked. "Don't ever forget that, Red. Clearly one of your suspects is lying about their alibi. Unless the real killer is someone we haven't yet considered."

I hoped that wasn't the case. It would be like starting over. But I couldn't think of anyone else who would benefit from Bud's death. The treasure hunters had left town, and no one else would have cared about the land but Charlie. Well, except for Minnie and Sophie. But surely those nice little old tea-drinking ladies couldn't be murderers, could they? What if they'd seen Steve and Bernie out there surveying the land and thought Bud was getting ready to sell out? Would they have gone as far as murder to keep the quiet neighborhood they were used to living in?

"Maybe Charlie was more worried about Bud selling out than the treasure hunters, and he set up that whole fake ghost thing to make the land less valuable," Moe suggested.

"What do you mean?"

"He told you he saw the surveyor out there, right?

And he'd heard the rumors of the pharmacy being built just like Minnie and Sophie had, right? Maybe he figured a big pharmacy company wouldn't want to build on that land if it was haunted. Maybe Bud caught him."

"But Charlie has someone that swears she was with him at the time of Bud's death. Then again, all my suspects do."

Moe scowled at me. "What, did you just fall off the cabbage truck? You ever heard of payoffs?"

"You mean Charlie paid someone to lie about his alibi."

"Yeah. And the others too."

"Come to think of it, Steve mentioned that Brent had paid people off before. He was worried Brent would somehow squelch the conservation land application he had going. That's why he was so secretive about it."

"Well, does Brent's car squeak? Don't forget, we never did discover where that banshee wailing that the neighbors heard came from."

"I never got a chance to check that out. Once Jinx overheard O'Hara confirm Brent's alibi at the Bubbling Cauldron, I didn't think it was that important."

Moe rolled his eyes. "Didn't I tell you, never drop investigating a suspect?"

He had. I should have at least checked the car to see if it squealed. But something didn't add up. Chastity had lied and said she was with Brent, and if he was the killer, then that meant the girlfriend and the bartender had lied also. Why would Brent pay off three people to lie and create confusing alibis for him?

I stared at the piece of plastic in my hand. It could definitely be from one of Charlie's vignettes. Then again, it was so small it could be from something else too. But it sure was a creepy hobby and obsession with murder that Charlie had. Maybe Bud's death had nothing to do with the treasure or pharmacies or land or kids fighting, and Charlie was just a wacko that liked to kill people.

My phone chimed on my desk with an angry text from Liz about how Julian had called to ask her to the Witch's Brew. I snorted out loud, waking Jinx, who had slipped into snore-sleep on the couch. I still owed Liz one from when she'd first set me up with Mitch all those years ago in high school, and now she was finding payback was a bitch.

While I was still looking at Liz's angry text, another one came in. This one was from Tess, confirming the manicure appointments for the next day. Tomorrow at ten a.m. Dang, Liz would probably try to get back at me before then, and I didn't doubt her focus would be on Joe Hayes, the chocolatier.

I put the phone away, the warm, fuzzy feelings of family camaraderie fading as I looked at the plastic piece.

In the background, Moe was rambling on about suspects and thoroughly checking alibis and how a shamus had to do his due diligence and not go off on assumption, but I was barely listening. My brain was churning on that little piece of plastic.

Suddenly, I shot up from my desk and grabbed my purse.

"Where are you going?" both Jinx and Moe asked at the same time.

"I know who the killer is, and I'm going to prove it."

CHAPTER NINETEEN

Brent and Chastity's house was dark. No car in the driveway. That was fine by me. I wasn't interested in looking at the car.

I parked down at the end of the street and skulked along the shrubs and hedges, thankful for the cover of darkness, as I made my way back to their house.

Luckily, it appeared that no one was home, so I could sneak in, verify my suspicions, and then get out before anyone even knew I was there.

"Are you breaking in?" Jinx asked as I held my lock-picking kit up to my face, making sure to choose the right tool for the lock.

"No."

"Yes, you are. That's against the law." So now he was interested in upholding the law?

The lock clicked, and I slowly pushed the door open. The smell of oil, mildew, and discarded memories hit me as I slipped inside. The garage was crowded with sagging, dust-covered boxes. Piled in the corners were cast-off snowshoes and skis. Rusted fishing poles hung from hooks on the walls. Christmas decorations poked out of the tops of a few boxes.

Over in the corner, something bulky huddled under a blue tarp. I headed toward it.

"What are you doing?" Jinx asked.

"Shhh. This is a covert operation. We don't want anyone to know we're here."

I knelt beside the tarp, dropping my bag within easy reach just in case I needed a chocolate. The tarp crinkled as I grabbed one end and slowly lifted it to reveal exactly what I had expected to see.

A scooter.

This one was purple, with a black padded seat and chrome handlebars. It looked like an older model, the kind that might have a squeaky belt.

At Bud's barn, Chastity had mentioned that she wanted to use the car because she had an appointment in town and it was too far for her to take the scooter. At the time, I'd been focusing on the fact that they only had one car, which meant only one of them could have left the house at a time. If one of them used the car, the other would have known, and if Brent was with his girlfriend, Chastity would have been at home. But Bud's house was less than a mile away from here. Close enough for her to take the scooter. Not to mention that Minnie had said she hadn't seen any cars, because the scooter had only one headlight, not two.

Now to figure out if this thing had a loose belt.

I made my way to the engine, tilting my head to look at it from all sides. It was hard to see because the garage was dark.

"So this is what made that banshee wailing noise." Jinx was at the back tire. I joined him, crouching to look at things from his angle. The scooter had purple splash guards over the tops of the tires, but this one had been dented. It was rubbing against the rubber tire. I pictured the belt on the vacuum at home. It had been rubbing against something metal too. Uncle Cosmo had said that's what made it squeal. Would this be enough to produce the noise Minnie and Sophie had mistaken for a ghost?

I could take a picture, but how in the world was I going to get Sheriff O'Hara on board with accepting this kind of a clue from me? She didn't even believe in ghosts. Not to mention that she'd dismiss anything I said. Maybe that nice Officer Parker who had been there when Aunt Gladys had been brought in would be more receptive. Hadn't cousin Tess mentioned him one time—

"Just what do you think you're doing in here?"

Oops, and here I'd thought no one was home.

I peered around the tire in the direction of the voice. The light spilling out from the open door highlighted the silhouette of a person. The backlighting made it impossible to see their features, but I didn't need more light to know who it was.

It was Chastity Saunders, and she had a gun pointed in my direction.

I raised my palms slowly. "Chastity, it's me, Jane Gallows."

"What are you doing to my scooter?"

"Nothing ..." Keep her talking. Wasn't that what I was supposed to do? My eyes flicked to my bag three feet away at the front of the scooter. Nestled inside were my chocolates. I didn't dare make a move toward it. If only I could get at those chocolates, I could cast a lights-out spell or maybe even a frozen-in-place spell to make her move slowly. But I couldn't get to the bag without risking getting shot.

"You couldn't leave well enough alone, could you?" Chastity said.

"What do you mean?" I played dumb. Maybe I could pretend she wasn't my number-one suspect as Bud's murderer. Though playing dumb probably wasn't going to work so well, considering I had just broken into her garage.

"You've been sniffing around my father-in-law's murder, digging up things that should not be dug up."

Odd choice of words, considering the whole treasure thing. "I'm not the only one that's been digging."

She stepped closer, holding the gun menacingly out in front of her. I spotted Jinx slipping behind an old box. Hiding? Or did he have something up his sleeve? I could hardly blame him for hiding. If one of us had to get shot, it should be me. I was bigger and could survive a bullet better. I was hoping to come up with a clever way out so that neither of us got shot though.

Maybe I could lull Chastity into a false sense of security by pretending to be sympathetic to her problems with Brent.

"Look, Chastity, I know what a louse your husband is. I'm sure everyone will understand that you couldn't take it anymore. I don't know why you killed Bud, but if it had something to do with Brent, I think a jury would be really sympathetic about that. Not so much if you shoot me though." Should I not have mentioned anything about her killing Bud? So much for playing dumb to get away.

I didn't know what I expected. Maybe for her to break down in tears or drop the gun and confess that she'd only done it because her husband was such a jerk. But that didn't happen. Instead, she seemed to grow colder. And closer. The gun was still aimed at me.

"That's right. Brent is a total jerk. I had to suffer and pretend to be the good wife because he held the purse strings. I couldn't escape. And then I found out about the treasure on Bud's property from one of those online forums. That's all I wanted—the money to get away from Brent."

"So it was you digging for the treasure?" This explained the conflicting reports I'd heard about Bud's relatives not bothering with him. According to what Bud had told people, they never visited. But some had reported seeing Chastity there, presumably to visit her father-in-law. Chastity *had* gone to Bud's, but not to visit. She'd been going there to dig for the treasure.

"Of course it was. Oh sure, there were some other people out there, and that crazy old coot next door kept coming over with his fake ghost act."

At my raised-eyebrow look, she smiled. "Oh yeah. I knew all about that. Who would believe there was a real ghost? Lucky for me, those treasure hunters were stupid, because it scared them off. Did you know that crazy old guy makes three-dimensional murder-scene art? He's nuttier than a fruitcake."

Jinx poked his head out from behind a box and caught my eye. I was still not sure what he was up to, but at least he had a plan.

"But why did you kill Bud?" Chastity seemed willing to talk, so I figured I might as well get a full confession.

"I didn't want to kill him." She stepped even closer. I tried to back up, but the cement wall was behind me. Once again I was caught on the floor, crouching, with someone looming over me. I made a mental note not to crouch so much. First, O'Hara had caught me at the tree, and now Chastity.

"Killing Bud was an accident," she continued, taking another step closer. Her red fingernail polish glittered in the light filtering in from the house.

Yep, my deduction had been correct. The plastic piece I had found where Bud's body had lain wasn't from Charlie's vignette, it was from Chastity's acrylic nails. I should have known the day I had run into her coming out of the nail salon when Lucy mentioned she came in almost every day. She had been going there for a similar reason to Aunt Gladys's. Her nails were chipped and dirty from digging.

"I kind of liked Bud. Killing him was an accident. He caught me digging around the barn. He was mad. He thought I was the one making all the ghost ruckus. I tried to reason with him. I even showed him the speakers and how the cord came from Charlie's. But he wouldn't hear any of it." Her face darkened. "We argued. I told him I had something awful to tell him about Brent. I didn't want anyone to overhear. It was so mortifying. So he agreed to go in the barn. I told him how awful Brent was to me and how I just wanted the money to get away."

"What did he say?"

"He wouldn't hear any of it. He thought Brent was the best thing since sliced bread. He grabbed my arm, and I pushed back. He fell backward onto the pitchfork." Remorse flickered across her face, but then she drew in a breath and her face turned cold again. "It was awful. You should have seen the look on his face."

I *had* seen the look. Apparently the ghastly look on Bud's face had been surprise and maybe a little bit of horror too. Surprise his daughter-in-law had pushed him and horror at the unfortunate placement of the pitchfork.

I could see Jinx sneaking around the perimeter of the garage, making his way toward me. I figured I had better keep Chastity talking so he could enact his plan. "And then what did you do?"

"I hightailed it out of there. I couldn't get caught with my father-in-law's body. Brent would make my life miserable if he knew I killed his dad, even if it was an accident. He'd hold it over me somehow."

"So that's why you went along with Brent's lie about being at home the night Bud died. It also provided *you* with an alibi." I had thought Brent seemed a little surprised when Chastity had corroborated his alibi that day. Later on, I figured maybe he'd paid her off and wasn't sure if she'd crack under the pressure of Sheriff O'Hara being there. But now I knew he actually really had been surprised. He hadn't expected Chastity to stick up for him.

Chastity laughed. "Yeah. Funny thing. For once his carousing actually worked in my favor."

"And you kept digging even after there was a murder investigation going on."

"Of course. I had to. Even more so now than ever. I had no idea if Brent would inherit money from his dad, but even if he did, he wouldn't give me any. And seeing as I'd killed Bud, I figured it would be smart to get out of town as fast as I could. But with no money, it's pretty hard to get out of town."

"I'm sure if you tell this same story to the police, the judge will be very sympathetic," I lied. "After all, it was just an accident."

Chastity laughed, a high-pitched shriek that didn't make me feel very confident about talking her out of killing me. "Nice try. Unfortunately, Jane, now that you know the truth, I'm going to have to make sure you never tell anyone. And it's so very convenient that you've taken the tarp off the scooter, since I'm going to wrap your body in it before I dispose of it." She waved the gun toward the tarp, which was now lying on the ground. "Go ahead, step on it. It'll make less of a mess if I shoot you right on it."

Before I could make a move, a scuffling sound and a guttural growl came from the front of the scooter, distracting Chastity. Her gaze swiveled in that direction.

Jinx was rummaging in my purse. He skewered

the bag of chocolates, flipping it into the air toward me. Chocolates rained down everywhere. Mocha creams. Vanilla creams. Malted milk balls. I caught a peanut butter cup mid-air, shoved it into my mouth, and chewed as if my life depended on it.

CHAPTER TWENTY

Chastity swung her gun in Jinx's direction.

"Hey, didn't anyone ever tell you it's not polite to point?" Jinx hissed at her, arching his back.

Chastity looked confused, her eyes darting from Jinx to the white bag to the chocolates, now scattered over the floor.

I knew I only had a few precious seconds to focus on the spell, which was unfortunate, because thinking up spells on the fly was not my forte. I didn't have time to peruse my mental Rolodex of enchantments for the most appropriate one, so I did the first one that came to mind. An irresistible-craving spell.

Chastity's eyes widened as she stared at the candy.

"Oh, are those maple creams?" Her gun clattered to the floor as she dove on the candy, picking up a handful and stuffing it into her mouth.

I raced over to the gun and picked it up then pointed it at her. Even though she was busy stuffing her face now, I didn't know how long the spell would last.

Then I did something I hated to do, especially twice in one week. I called Sheriff Bobby O'Hara.

O'Hara showed up five minutes later in a whir of sirens and a blaze of lights, looking more disappointed that I wasn't the killer than happy that I had caught the person who was.

"And just what were you doing here, Gallows?" she asked as Officer Parker led Chastity away. Chastity had confessed easily, especially when I bribed her with candy. The only problem came when O'Hara tried to snap on the cuffs. Chastity had resisted because she was still shoving candy into her mouth, and the cuffs impeded her eating. The only downside to the whole thing was that I'd have to resupply; she'd eaten all the chocolate. Well, that and the fact that I was now stuck explaining to O'Hara.

"Like I told you, I was still investigating Bud's death because he hired me. I just wanted to see the case through to the end," I said.

"Uh huh. And you were in the garage because ..."

"I suspected Brent and Chastity had lied about their alibi."

"Yeah, any amateur could have seen that," O'Hara said as if justifying why she hadn't been in the garage looking for clues.

"Right. So Minnie Wheeler and Sophie Liberty thought they heard a car squealing the night Bud was killed."

"Uh huh..." O'Hara looked confused, as if she didn't know where I was going with this.

"So I just came over to see if Brent and Chastity's car squealed."

O'Hara walked over to the door, checking the lock, apparently to see if it had been jimmied. "Yeah, so how did you end up in the garage with the homeowner holding a gun on you?"

"Oh. Well, I was gonna just do some surveillance, but then I heard a noise coming from the garage, and I came to investigate."

"How did you get in?"

"The door was unlocked." No way was I going to admit to picking the lock and give her ammunition to pull me into the station.

"So what happened once you came in?"

I gestured toward the few chocolates that were left on the floor. "I guess maybe some mice had gotten in here and knocked over some boxes and were rummaging around for food. Anyway, Chastity must have heard the same commotion and come out to investigate with her gun."

"And she found you here, uncovering her scooter?" O'Hara's tone was skeptical.

"Well, yeah. See, when I came in to investigate, I noticed a mouse over by the tarp. I was trying to get rid of it when the tarp slid off the scooter, and I realized this could be the vehicle that had been wailing the night Bud was killed."

"Uh huh. And then you conveniently got her to confess?"

I shrugged. "Yeah. I mean, it just all came bubbling out. You heard her yourself."

"Was she drunk or on drugs or something?" O'Hara looked back toward the police car, where Parker was trying to stuff Chastity into the back. "She seems a little loopy, and she keeps begging for chocolate."

I nodded. "I think that's it. She must be on something. That's why she confessed so easily."

O'Hara stared at me for a long moment then put her notebook away. "Okay. I guess that sums it up then, Gallows. I had her at the top of my suspect list, and we were just closing in on her anyway, so don't go putting on airs about how your amateur detecting caught the killer before the police."

"Oh, I wouldn't dream of it. Can I go now?"

"Yep. And if you want, you can feel free to leave town."

I wanted to go straight home after O'Hara let me go, but I figured I owed it to Moe to fill him in on what had happened. I was feeling pretty good about myself, having discovered the killer and gotten her to confess.

I figured the mill building would be empty, but there was a light on in the office on the first floor. As we approached, the door opened. I was finally going to meet the mysterious new occupant.

I was a little excited. The mill building was kind of boring. Maybe the new person was someone interesting that would liven up my day.

A familiar figure stepped out the door. No. It couldn't be. That was when I noticed the black-and-gold sign on top of the door. Mitch Pierce.

"Oh, no. Don't tell me he's the new neighbor." Jinx disliked Mitch even more than I did.

I stared at Mitch, my mouth agape. His lips quirked in a knowing smile. He'd moved here on purpose.

"Don't tell me this is your office," I sputtered, gesturing wildly toward his door.

"Yep." His eyes dropped to Jinx. "Don't tell me you're still dragging that flea-bitten, smelly old thing around."

"Hey, I'm not flea-bitten and I don't smell," Jinx hissed.

"No. This is some kind of a joke. Why would you move into my building when you had a prestigious office downtown?"

"Turns out that a lot of clients prefer it when a private investigator is in a much sleazier location. I heard a few of them saying they were going to check out your business because the mill seemed like a place a detective that didn't mind getting his hands dirty would work out of. So I figured if you can't beat them, join them. Besides, I kind of miss seeing your smiling face every day."

What a jerk. "Well, I don't have a lot of clients, so you made a bad move. You should move back to your nice office before they rent it to someone else."

Mitch's charming smile tugged at my traitorous heartstrings. I would not fall under his spell again. If I had some chocolate, I'd cast a steer-clear spell on myself.

"Oh, come on, Sunshine, it will be fun being in

the same building. Maybe we can even work some cases together."

I'd rather eat worms. I hitched my bag up on my shoulder and jerked my door open. "I highly doubt that."

I stormed up the steps, Jinx at my side.

"I hate it when he calls me Sunshine," I mumbled.

"I hate it when he calls me old, flea-bitten, and smelly," Jinx said.

My blood was boiling by the time I reached my office. The nerve of him getting an office right below mine! And all because he thought he'd get more clients. So now this meant he was going to start taking clients from *me*. I'd have to work doubly hard, and I sure as heck wasn't going to be as picky as I had been. From here on in, I was going to accept every client that came my way, just like Moe had suggested.

I jerked the door open, disturbing Moe, who had been lying on the couch.

"Red! What's going on? I was trying to get some shuteye. That bird downstairs has been making a lot of noise today. How does he expect a guy to sleep? I don't think I'm going to like having him here if he's that noisy."

"You and me both." I wondered how I could get

rid of Mitch. Could I cast some kind of spell on him? Maybe a gone-fishing spell or a retirement spell? My spells never lasted, but I was sure my cousins would help me out.

"You must have some news. You don't come here at night unless something's going on," Moe said.

"As a matter of fact, I do. The case is solved."

Moe clapped his hands, a smile cracking his face. "That's great news!"

He turned to the corner he often materialized from. I pictured he must have some sort of a ghost apartment back there, because he often came out with different clothes, cards, hats.

When he turned back around, he was holding up a bottle of whiskey. "I say we celebrate." He pulled a shot glass out of his pocket and poured some of the amber liquid into it then held it out toward me.

I lifted my hand to accept before realizing I couldn't imbibe his ghostly spirits. Which was a shame, because I could have really used a drink.

"Oh yeah. I forgot you can't drink. More for me." He downed the shot and poured another before plopping onto the couch. "Oh. Before I forget. Someone was here pounding on the door. Sounded real urgent."

"Probably the noisy neighbor downstairs. Or

maybe Hightower. Or it could have been that lady from the paper. Either way, I'm sure they can wait."

"I don't know. Didn't sound like they could wait," Moe said. "Judging by the way they were pounding on the door, I got the impression it might have been someone seeking our investigative services."

"Oh, really?" That might be a good sign. If someone was coming up here to hire us, they would have had to walk right past Mitch's sign. Maybe things wouldn't be so bad after all.

"Well, hopefully they'll come back tomorrow." Moe patted the couch beside him. "Now sit down and tell me all about how we solved the case."

CHAPTER TWENTY-ONE

I took the next morning off. I'd spent a few hours filling Moe in on the exciting capture of Chastity the night before and left him clutching his whiskey bottle and snoozing on the couch. We'd worked hard, and I figured we both deserved the morning off. Hopefully the persistent client wouldn't come back until I returned.

It was a gloriously warm day, the kind of late-summer day on which the air is tinged with a bitter-sweet end-of-summer nostalgia mingled with the smell of freshly mown grass. We were lounging out by the pool after just having had our nails done. Pink for Liz, purple sparkles for Tess and Gladys, scarlet for Wanda. Being even more practical than Liz, I had gone for clear. I'd just finished giving them a dramatic rendition of capturing Chastity.

"See, your magic is powerful, dear." Aunt Gladys put her hand on my arm. "You managed to disarm a cold-blooded killer with it."

Even though I knew my magic wasn't really that powerful, my family had always gone out of their way to make it seem like it was so that I didn't feel "less than." The truth was, I was pretty proud that I'd captured Chastity. Even better, I'd figured out who the killer was and gotten her to confess without even using an ounce of magic until the very end when I needed to keep her from shooting me.

"Ahem!"

We all turned to see Jinx staring up at us with a perturbed look on his face.

"I helped."

"Yes, you were a big help." It was true. Without Jinx, I wouldn't have been able to get to the chocolates. I shuddered to think what might have happened if he hadn't been there.

"Yeah, and what about how I discovered that the tire was rubbing?" Jinx asked. "That was pivotal to cracking the case."

"Right. You did do that."

"And the digging over at Bud's. I found that too."

"Yeah. I guess you are a pretty big help. Maybe

you should start your own private investigator business."

"You know, that's not such a bad idea, because I also discovered that—"

"Jinxy," Aunt Wanda cut in. Good thing, too, because I could tell Jinx was about to go on one of his self-indulgent rants about how important he was. "You want some catnip? It's fresh from my garden."

Jinx whipped his head around. "Say what? You have fresh catnip? Is it that special blend? You know, the stuff from the seeds you got in Colombia."

"One and the same." Wanda pulled a purple velvet bag out of her pocket, pinched out some dried herbs, and scattered them on the patio.

Jinx pounced on the herbs, flipped onto his back, then wiggled around, his feet kicking up in the air.

"That ought to occupy him for a while," Tess said.

A rustle in the bushes near the wrought iron fence caught my eye. "Someone's out there."

Aunt Wanda glanced in that direction. "Oh, that's just Harvey, the gardener."

We all watched as Harvey appeared in view on the lawnmower. He was shirtless, showing off tanned, rippling muscles.

"Wanda, the poison ivy spell," Aunt Gladys

reminded. "We don't want Harvey to get a rash and ruin all that nice … skin."

Wanda sighed. "Unfortunately, I had to do a disenchantment on that. Harvey needs to get out there and mow a clear path to the jack-o-lantern patch. I need to make sure there are enough mature ones for Old Coven Days."

My eyes drifted out to the large green patch dotted with orange orbs. Some of the jack-o-lanterns were already glowing. Aunt Wanda was in charge of decorating for Old Coven Days, and she planned to line the perimeters of the hexagon with jack-o-lanterns from the garden. As I watched, one turned toward us, an alarmed expression on its face. My chest constricted for the jack-o-lanterns. Despite their gap-toothed smiles and brightly lit eyes, they hated being picked. Jack-o-lanterns had a great life in the patch, but once they had been plucked, their days were numbered.

"So I guess Mrs. Newman will be coming back to spy on us," Liz said, her gaze drifting off into the distance toward Newman's house.

"I don't know if she'll be coming back anytime soon," I said. "I saw her coming out of the pharmacy yesterday, and she was itching like crazy. Had a bag loaded up with something. Calamine lotion, I assume."

"Serves her right," Tess said, admiring the way her nails sparkled in the sunlight.

"At least Hightower stopped threatening us," Wanda said.

Aunt Gladys made a clucking sound. "I wish. She's still stalking me. I went down to Bruno's Market yesterday, and she followed me all around the store. Oh, she pretended like she wasn't, but I could tell, because she ended up in every aisle I was in, and her cart was empty. And when I got to the housewares aisle, she strategically placed herself in front of the brooms as if she were guarding them."

"She can be very annoying," Liz said.

"As if I was going to take her precious brooms." Aunt Gladys spread her hands to indicate all the brooms on the patio. "I think I have enough."

"She'll never stop bothering us as long as she thinks our unconventional behavior might scare tourists away," Wanda said. "Funny thing is, I think our unconventional behavior plays right into the spirit of the town."

"She's just got a grudge against us," Gladys said. "Might have to do with the fact that Rocky Dickson chose to go to the town fair with me instead of her."

Wanda frowned. "That was fifteen years ago."

Gladys shrugged. "Some people hold a grudge."

"So how is the brooming going?" Wanda asked Glad.

Glad's face fell. "Not so good. I guess it was silly of me to think it was all because of defective brooms. It really is something wrong with me. I'm the one that is defective."

Wanda's face softened, and she put her hand on Gladys's. "You're not defective, honey. Maybe you're just having a bad spell. You know, like when you have a cold or the flu or something. I think your magic will come back."

"I don't know…." Glad looked so sad it made my heart twist.

"I could make you another potion, but you have to promise not to guzzle the whole thing down," Tess said. "What is the problem, anyway?"

"I'll show you." Gladys stood. Thrusting her hands out at one of the brooms—a red one this time—she wiggled her fingers and yelled, "Shazbot!"

The broom wiggled and waggled, flopping around on the patio like a fish, then finally it rose into the air and hovered, as if waiting to be called.

Gladys stuck two fingers in her mouth and gave a wolf whistle. The broom zoomed over toward her, coming to a stop in front of her, as if beckoning for her to get on. But as soon as she moved toward it, it backed up out of her reach. She stepped toward it again. It backed up again, and then it went totally vertical, dropped to the ground, and started sweeping the patio.

Gladys slumped into her chair. "See? My enchantments are all messed up. Instead of enchanting the brooms into flying, they end up sweeping."

"Well, Zelda might like that," Wanda said.

We sat there silently, watching the broom as it made its way over to Jinx, who was still rolling in the catnip. It started trying to sweep up the catnip, swatting Jinx in the process.

"Hey, what the ..." Jinx sprang up and batted at the broom. The broom batted back. Jinx hissed and struck out with his paw. The broom advanced. Jinx backed up, swatting and hissing. It was like some kind of weird dance.

Wanda tore her eyes away first. "Well, what are you going to do, Gladys? Your license expires soon, and you wanted to ride in the Old Coven Days parade."

Gladys slouched even lower in her seat, her expression turning even more glum. "I don't know."

Her brows knitted together as she glared at the broom. "I may just have to do something drastic."

We exchanged disturbed glances. The last time Gladys had done something drastic, the whole town had started acting crazy. Hopefully it wouldn't come to that.

"Speaking of drastic," Liz said. "I saw that Mitch moved into your building."

"Yeah, I discovered that last night. Not happy," I said.

Tess frowned. "Is he trying to take your clients? I could zap him with a spinach-stuck-in-teeth spell, or maybe an I'm-too-lazy-to-work enchantment."

"You know we're not supposed to fool with the lives of humans with our spells and enchantments, though I do appreciate the sentiment."

"I think he's trying to get you back," Liz said.

No! "I doubt that."

"Oh, by the way. Did you hear from Charming Chocolates?" Liz asked.

Warning bells immediately sounded in my head. "No. Why? What did you do?"

She waved her hand dismissively. "Oh, nothing bad. Really. I'm just sending you a little gift to thank you for fixing me up with Julian."

Was she joking? Had she really hit it off with

Julian and was thanking me? Or was this some kind of punishment? My mind whirled. What could it be? Almond bark? Chocolate fudge? No. Judging by the smug look in her eyes, I had a feeling her gift had less to do with chocolates and more to do with the delicious chocolatier. But what could it be? Something embarrassing, no doubt.

"Don't worry, Jane. After word gets out about how successful you were in capturing Bud Saunders's killer, clients will be knocking down your door. I wouldn't worry about that nasty Mitch Pierce," Aunt Wanda said.

"Yeah. That's right, Wanda," Gladys said. "I wouldn't even be surprised if Sheriff O'Hara herself asked Jane to consult on the latest murder."

"Latest murder?" we all asked.

Aunt Gladys chewed on her nail. "You didn't hear?"

"No."

"Oh, well, er ... A dead body was found late last night down at the barber shop."

Wanda turned to her. "And just how do you know that?"

Aunt Gladys blanched and waved her hand in the air dismissively. "I heard about it down at the market."

"The market isn't open late at night." Wanda glared at Gladys. "I hope this doesn't have something to do with you whooping it up at the Witch's Brew Lounge or being arrested in the park."

"No. Not at all. That was all because I drank the potion. I'm over that now that it's out of my system." *Hiccup.*

Wanda sighed. "I hope so. You know how Hightower is. If she thinks you had anything to do with a murder, she will be relentless."

"Oh, no worries. I have an alibi."

"Moe did say someone was practically trying to knock down my office door last night. He thought it was a desperate client," I said. Even though I didn't tell regular people about the ghost in my office, my own family was well versed in the paranormal and thought nothing of ghosts in offices, or skeletons in closets for that matter.

"Wonderful! Then it looks like you got another client. See, the clients are coming right to you. No need to worry about that nasty Mitch Pierce."

Right. No need to worry. The client would have had to have walked right by Mitch's fancy-pants sign to get to my office. So surely they wanted my services and not Mitch's. And just because the potential client had been relentlessly pounding at my office door shortly before a mysterious body was found in the barber shop wasn't any reason to worry. Was it?

****

Sign up for my newsletter to get my latest releases at the lowest discount price and I'll send you a never before published novella in my Lexy Baker series:

http://www.leighanndobbs.com/newsletter

If you want to receive a text message alert on your cell phone for new releases , text COZYMYSTERY to 88202 (sorry, this only works for US cell phones!)

Join my readers group on Facebook and get sneak peeks at my latest books:

https://www.facebook.com/groups/ldobbsreaders/

ALSO BY LEIGHANN DOBBS

Cozy Mysteries

Silver Hollow

Paranormal Cozy Mystery Series

***

A Spell of Trouble (Book 1)

Spell Disaster (Book 2)

Nothing to Croak About (Book 3)

Cry Wolf (Book 4)

Blackmoore Sisters

Cozy Mystery Series

* * *

Dead Wrong

Dead & Buried

Dead Tide

Buried Secrets

Deadly Intentions

A Grave Mistake

Spell Found

Fatal Fortune

Kate Diamond Mystery Adventures

***

Hidden Agemda (Book 1)

Ancient Hiss Story (Book 2)

Heist Society (Book 3)

Mooseamuck Island Cozy Mystery Series

* * *

A Zen For Murder

A Crabby Killer

A Treacherous Treasure

Mystic Notch

Cat Cozy Mystery Series

* * *

Ghostly Paws

A Spirited Tail

A Mew To A Kill

Paws and Effect

Probable Paws

Lexy Baker Cozy Mystery Series

* * *

Lexy Baker Cozy Mystery Series Boxed Set Vol 1 (Books 1-4)

Or buy the books separately:

Killer Cupcakes

Dying For Danish

Murder, Money and Marzipan

3 Bodies and a Biscotti

Brownies, Bodies & Bad Guys

Bake, Battle & Roll

Wedded Blintz

Scones, Skulls & Scams

Ice Cream Murder

Mummified Meringues

Brutal Brulee (Novella)

No Scone Unturned

Cream Puff Killer

Hazel Martin Historical Mystery Series

***

Murder at Lowry House (book 1)

Murder by Misunderstanding (book 2)

Lady Katherine Regency Mysteries

***

An Invitation to Murder (Book 1)

The Baffling Burglaries of Bath (Book 2)

Sam Mason Mysteries

(As L. A. Dobbs)

***

Telling Lies (Book 1)

Keeping Secrets (Book 2)

Exposing Truths (Book 3)

Betraying Trust (Book 4)

Romantic Comedy

***

Corporate Chaos Series

In Over Her Head (book 1)

Can't Stand the Heat (book 2)

What Goes Around Comes Around (book 3)

Contemporary Romance

***

Reluctant Romance

Sweet Romance (Written As Annie Dobbs)

Firefly Inn Series

***

Another Chance (Book 1)

Another Wish (Book 2)

Hometown Hearts Series

***

No Getting Over You (Book 1)

A Change of Heart (Book 2)

***

Sweetrock Sweet and Spicy Cowboy Romance

Some Like It Hot

Too Close For Comfort

———

Regency Romance

* * *

Scandals and Spies Series:

Kissing The Enemy

Deceiving the Duke

Tempting the Rival

Charming the Spy

Pursuing the Traitor

Captivating the Captain

The Unexpected Series:

An Unexpected Proposal

An Unexpected Passion

Dobbs Fancytales:

Dobbs Fancytales Boxed Set Collection

Western Historical Romance

***

Goldwater Creek Mail Order Brides:

Faith

American Mail Order Brides Series:

Chevonne: Bride of Oklahoma

Magical Romance with a Touch of Mystery

***

Something Magical

Curiously Enchanted

ROMANTIC SUSPENSE

WRITING AS LEE ANNE JONES:

***

The Rockford Security Series:

Deadly Betrayal (Book 1)

Fatal Games (Book 2)

Treacherous Seduction (Book 3)

Calculating Desires (Book 4)

Wicked Deception (Book 5)

ABOUT LEIGHANN DOBBS

USA Today bestselling author, Leighann Dobbs, discovered her passion for writing after a twenty year career as a software engineer. She lives in New Hampshire with her husband Bruce, their trusty Chihuahua mix Mojo and beautiful rescue cat, Kitty. When she's not reading, gardening, making jewelry or selling antiques, she likes to write cozy mystery and historical romance books.

Her book "Dead Wrong" won the "Best Mystery Romance" award at the 2014 Indie Romance Convention.

Her book "Ghostly Paws" was the 2015 Chanticleer Mystery & Mayhem First Place category winner in the Animal Mystery category.

Find out about her latest books by signing up at:

http://www.leighanndobbs.com/newsletter

Connect with Leighann on Facebook
http://facebook.com/leighanndobbsbooks

Join her VIP readers group on Facebook:
https://www.facebook.com/groups/ldobbsreader
s/

This is a work of fiction.

None of it is real. All names, places, and events are products of the author's imagination. Any resemblance to real names, places, or events are purely coincidental, and should not be construed as being real.

The Case of the Sinister Spirit

Leighann Dobbs Publishing

http://www.leighanndobbs.com

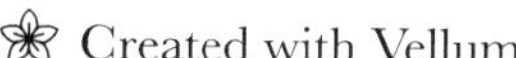

Made in the USA
Coppell, TX
13 October 2021

64017895R00136